J

W9-BYF-027

STACKS

DEBBIE DOESN'T DO IT ANYMORE

WALTER MOSLEY

THORNDIKE PRESS

A part of Gale, Cengage Learning

GALE
CENGAGE Learning·

Farmington Hills, Mich · San Francisco · New York · Waterville, Maine
Meriden, Conn · Mason, Ohio · Chicago

GALE
CENGAGE Learning®

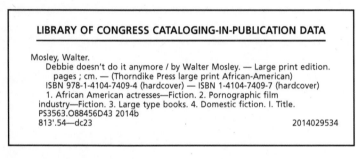

LIBRARY OF CONGRESS CATALOGING-IN-PUBLICATION DATA

Mosley, Walter.
  Debbie doesn't do it anymore / by Walter Mosley. — Large print edition.
    pages ; cm. — (Thorndike Press large print African-American)
    ISBN 978-1-4104-7409-4 (hardcover) — ISBN 1-4104-7409-7 (hardcover)
    1. African American actresses—Fiction. 2. Pornographic film industry—Fiction. 3. Large type books. 4. Domestic fiction. I. Title.
  PS3563.O88456D43 2014b
  813'.54—dc23   2014029534

Published in 2014 by arrangement with Doubleday, an imprint of Knopf Doubleday Publishing Group, a division of Random House, LLC, a Penguin Random House Company

Printed in Mexico
1 2 3 4 5 6 7 18 17 16 15 14

DEBBIE DOESN'T DO IT ANYMORE

I was reclining on my backside, thighs spread wide open. The smell of flower-scented lubricant filled the air, and hot lights burned down on my sweat-slick black skin. Blubbery and pink-skinned Myron "Big Dick" Palmer was slamming his thing into me, saying, "Oh, baby. Yeah, baby. Daddy's comin' home. He's almost there, almost there." There were two high-def video cameramen working us: one moving from face to face while the other focused on our genitals. The still photographer was Carmen Alia from Brazil. The recycling hum of her digital camera buzzed around us like a hungry horsefly circling an open wound.

"More passion!" Linda Love, the director, yelled.

She was talking to me. Myron always had the same passion in any sex scene because he closed his eyes and imagined that he was with Nora Brathwait, his high school sweet-

7

heart. She had never let him go all the way and every sex scene he ever did was dedicated to wiping that humiliation from his heart.

Luckily for me Myron's size pushed his thing against a sore spot deep inside. So when Linda called for more feeling I stopped thinking about the details of the shoot and began to concentrate on how much he was hurting me with his attempt to penetrate all the way back to adolescence.

I allowed the pain to show in my face with each stabbing lunge.

"That's better," Linda said.

"Almost there," Myron moaned for what seemed like the hundredth time. "Uh-uh."

The grunting meant that he was about to orgasm. I knew it, Myron knew it, and, worst of all, Linda was aware of what was coming — so to speak.

Within the next six seconds she'd cry, "On your knees, Debbie," and I'd have to jump down while looking up into the bright lights as Myron Big Dick ejaculated on my face and breasts.

That was the money shot, the reason I woke up at five a.m., spent hours doing makeup and hair, toes and fingers; it was the reason I'd capped my front teeth, had breast implants, worked out two hours a day five days a week with trainer-to-the-stars Efron Fuentes, and shaved my pussy more often than my husband shaved his chin.

The money shot was not only my paycheck but the salary of every grip, cameraman, makeup artist, and gofer in the room. Our reason for living would spout from Myron Palmer's big pink dick.

This was no revelation. I had experienced thousands of ejaculations from men of every color, size, and nationality. I had been spouted upon in Moscow, Kingston, Paris, and Johannesburg. This was my job, and the only thing I worried about was keeping the acrid stuff out of my eyes.

I was preparing to slide down from the sofa onto my knees when something amazing happened.

Myron grunted and Carmen switched to a double flash setting, Linda cried, "Debbie . . ." and Myron plunged up against the one spot in my entire sex that still had sensation. I could feel a blast from the air conditioner and the crusty fabric of the sofa where we teetered, me on my back wearing only leopard-print high-high heels and Myron on his knees thrusting, thrusting. And then, completely unbidden, I imagined a tall, olive-skinned man with intense eyes standing in the corner of the crowded room. I knew this man but could not name him. I was moving toward him and at the same time I was being stalked by the most powerful orgasm that I'd ever experienced. The faster I moved the closer the feeling came until suddenly I was bucking and screaming, begging for more.

". . . on your knees!" Linda shouted, but I was way beyond taking orders from her. I could feel my nipples getting so tight that they seemed to be pinching themselves, and I felt the full weight of the experience of every one of my thirty-one years.

Myron pushed me off the red sofa and onto the floor. Then he stood up, drizzling his semen on me while I jerked around like a mackerel just landed on the deck of a day boat off San Pedro.

I wanted to stop but the orgasm was relentless, like a series of storm-driven waves crashing down on the shore. The only option open to me was to let go of consciousness while Linda and her producers tried to figure a way to save the shot and all our paychecks.

I woke up in what was once the nursery of the Bel-Air mansion. The owner of the house had been a movie producer for one of the big studios until his star waned. He foolishly mortgaged his house to finance his girlfriend's film, *Fun for Fauna.* The movie didn't even make it to DVD and now the owner, Sherman Pettigrew, rented his place for porno shoots whenever he could. Sherman lived in a trailer behind his ex-girlfriend's new beau's house in Topanga Canyon.

Anyway . . . I came awake on a daybed in the barren nursery of the failed movie producer's house, stillborn into wakefulness after wasting what seemed like the last iota of passion in my life.

"You okay?" a soft voice asked.

I raised my head and saw Lana Leer sitting on a pink wicker chair. She was very petite, very white, with hair as short as a new recruit's buzz cut.

"I passed out," I said.

"Yeah."

"It's so embarrassing."

Lana giggled. Then she laughed.

"What's so funny?" I asked even though I knew the answer.

"I don't mean to make fun, Deb, but it is kinda silly for a woman who's had sex with five men at once to be shy about an orgasm."

"Where is everybody?"

"They left. Linda asked me to stay and make sure you were all right but I would have anyway."

I realized that it was dark outside. When I shifted in the bed I felt the long-lasting slick lubricant between my thighs.

"How long was I out?"

"A long time."

"Was Linda mad?"

"No. Myron really saved the day. You looked good with him standing over you like that. It looked real."

"I have to get home, Lana," I said, trying to gather the strength to sit upright. "Has anybody heard from my husband?"

Linda reached out and took my hands. She remained steady and I was able to pull myself up.

"No. I called the house but only got the service."

"Thanks for staying with me. I remember once in Jamaica that dickhead Lester Foley got me high and left me in a hut on the beach without any clothes."

"Let's get you cleaned up," the diminutive personal assistant said.

There were three police cars, their red and blue lights flashing angrily, parked on the sidewalk, the lawn, and up in the driveway

12

of our home on South Elm in Pasadena.

Lana and I were walking up the slight incline of the lawn headed for the front door when someone said, "Excuse me, ladies; this is a possible crime scene and we're not allowing anyone in."

He was a small man in a black uniform with blue eyes and pink skin. He recognized me from his porno collection; I could see it in those startled eyes. There aren't many black-skinned women with long white hair and deep blue contact lenses. Debbie Dare was almost unique in the capital of a clichéd profession.

"Aren't you —" he began to ask.

"The owner of this house," I said. "What crime has possibly been committed?"

"Wait here, ma'am," he said, and I knew the news had to be bad.

Lana put a hand on my shoulder. It felt so heavy that I almost fell down. My legs were still weak from the unwanted orgasm and now this.

The uniform called into the front door of my house. A few seconds later a slender man in a cheap dark green suit came out. He traded a few words with the cop, looked in our direction, and, hesitantly I thought, walked toward us.

13

"Mrs. Pinkney?" he asked, looking at Lana.

"Yes," Lana said, "this is Mrs. Pinkney."

"Your husband, ma'am," he said, shifting his gaze to me.

He had passive, maybe even kind eyes and if he recognized me that fact was hidden behind an honest attempt at sympathy.

"What about him?"

The plainclothes cop tilted his head to the side and I couldn't help but think that that was the way he spoke to his mother when he'd been bad and had to come to her to confess the breaking of a water glass or leaving a door open, allowing the family pet to escape.

"He expired," the policeman said.

"Expired?" Lana asked.

"Died."

"Oh my God," Lana said, and then she began to cry.

"I'm so sorry," he said.

The news hit me like a bucket of cold water. Finally the intensity of my session with Myron was flushed away.

"I want to see him," I said.

The electricity was out in the house. Yellow metal stalks with powerful incandescent lamps, brought in by the police, eerily illuminated the sunken all-white living room and the double-wide hall that went past Theon's bedroom and mine. There was an even stronger light coming from the master bathroom. I could see the shadows of people moving around in there, mumbling words that I couldn't quite make out.

"Maybe you shouldn't see him like this," the plainclothes cop said at the door.

"What's your name?" I asked him.

"Lieutenant Mendelson."

"Your first name."

"Perry."

"Is that short for something?"

"I was named after Perry Como. My mother loved his voice."

"Are you married, Perry?"

"Yes. Of, of course." He said these last three words showing me the wedding band on his left hand.

"If it was your wife in there would you walk away because some stranger told you to?"

The policeman looked down and I instantly liked him. He took a step back and I walked into the huge bathroom.

There were three men and two women in there, all of them wearing blue hairnets and thin rubber gloves. One man was vacuuming the floor with a handheld device while another, a black woman, was taking photographs with a digital camera — bringing Carmen Alia to my mind.

I was further reminded of a porno shoot when I saw the inhabitants of our wide, baby blue circular bathtub.

My husband, Theon Pinkney, was naked on his back with his big belly up above the waterline. His left arm was around Jolie Wins, a sixteen-year-old wannabe adult cinema star.

Jolie was my polar opposite with her black hair and pale white skin. She didn't look dead.

There was a high-end video camera submerged at the far side of the tub. It was plugged into a wall and had tumbled into the impromptu sex scene that they were filming.

Theon had been a major star in the porn world before he was my husband. He called himself Axel Rod. After he got fat he became a somewhat successful manager before the stars and directors wrested their careers from producers, agents, and managers. Theon probably told Jolie that this was an audition, and he plugged in the camera because the battery had gone dead while he fucked her for hours.

Theon had lost his physical appeal but he

could keep up an erection longer than any man I'd ever met.

"Mrs. Pinkney?" Lieutenant Perry Mendelson said.

"Yes?"

There was the sound of a grunting moan in the background. Again I was reminded of my work.

"Are you all right?" the policeman asked.

"Why are the police here, Perry?"

"People have died."

"But it looks like an accident. Do you think he was murdered?"

"No," he said. "The way we see it the girl's foot got tangled in the wire and, and, and when she . . ."

"When she moved to get on top of him the camera fell in," I said.

"Yes."

"Then why is half the Pasadena police department in my home?"

"Your housekeeper, Mrs. Julia Slatkin, came in and found them. She called nine-one-one and said that it was murder. When someone claims foul play we are legally obligated to do an initial investigation."

"I see."

"Is this your husband?"

"Yes, it is."

"The housekeeper already ID'd him but

17

I'm required to ask."

"Where is Julia?"

"She was distraught. I had one of my men drive her home. Do you know the girl, Mrs. Pinkney?"

"No," I lied. "No, I don't. Who is she?"

"We didn't find any identification in her purse."

"She looks like a child. My husband was having sex with a child."

Perry Mendelson looked into my eyes and saw a blank slate. I turned away and went to Lana. She was on the floor in the hall, grunting and moaning, crying with an abandon I rarely felt.

I went to her and hunkered down. It was a familiar movement, a sex position without a partner.

I smiled.

"It's okay, baby," I said. And then to Perry, who was standing above us, "How long is this investigation going to last?"

"We can wrap it up in a couple of hours. I'll have some questions but they can wait until tomorrow if you don't feel up to it right now."

"That would be great. I'm an early riser. And, Perry?"

"Yes?"

"If you don't think it's a crime you can

have them take Theon's body to Threadley Brothers Mortuary. There's somebody there all night."

That night Lana and I lay side by side on white satin sheets under black cashmere blankets. I didn't really need the company, but Lana was a delicate girl and too upset to drive herself home.

She snored softly and pressed against me. I didn't sleep much but that wasn't unusual. I hadn't had a full night's rest in many years. It wasn't that I was sad or even insomniac. I just didn't seem to need that much sleep. Usually when Theon and I were both home he'd have sex with me and then drop off. For most of the night I'd read books at random, napping at odd times between chapters or sections; sometimes I'd even nod off in the middle of a sentence.

Over the years I read Tolstoy and Tennyson, Mary Higgins Clark and John Updike, Roger Zelazny and Octavia Butler in the early, early hours of the morning. I didn't finish as many books as some because I usually put down a story I didn't like and reread, many times over, those that I enjoyed.

If Theon woke up and found me reading he'd usually fuck me again. That was his talent — he could have sex anytime with anyone. If he didn't like burritos and cheesecake so much he could have been a porn star up into his seventies.

But the reason he had sex didn't have to do with love or the physical passion I'd felt that afternoon with Myron. Sex for Theon always had a definite purpose, like when he'd drowsily awake and see me reading. I was a herd mare and he was an aging stallion running with all his might to keep up.

I'd lie under him or get on my knees and move perfectly with his thrusts and withdrawals. After he'd come I'd turn him on his side and scrape his skin with my fake nails and bite his shoulders. And after a while he'd fall back to sleep and I'd pick up my book again.

Theon and I loved each other, I suppose. I knew him better than anyone else did and he never hit me. He had sex with other women all the time and I was free to do what I wanted, but that wasn't very often, not really. I wasn't worried about losing him, because sex was just a release or a means to an end for him. Theon told me that he didn't want me falling in love with another man, or woman. I told him that he didn't have to worry.

He was especially concerned that I didn't

fall in love with a black man. He was white and believed that the races tended to stay together and so felt threatened whenever I spent any time with any of my African American costars.

That night, after Theon's ridiculous death, lying there next to Lana — her rough breath like hope or something — I wanted to read but didn't have the strength to sit up or even reach over to the night table where *Dead Souls* was sitting, waiting for me to reread it for the seventh, or maybe eighth time.

A university professor I dated for a while told me that I was just a recreational reader, way outside of the educational system he lived in.

"You only talk about phrases and what the characters are feeling but you have no notion of the literary ideas or intentions," he said one night after I'd untied him. "You'd be lost in one of my classes. If I hadn't talked to you like this I wouldn't have believed that there was a literate thought in your head."

"But aren't your classes about what people in books say and feel?" I asked, as if I were making an appeal in a higher court.

"No," he said. "The study of literature today is about structure and underlying intention; it's about the way in which the themes of literature, historically, resonate with one another."

I stopped answering his calls after that. Professor Abraham was of no use to me if his world and mine were unconnected. We were, I thought, like two islands so close that one could see the other in great detail but the life evolving on each was separated by aeons of evolution.

I loved books and their stories and characters. Books were faithful and true in ways that real people could never be.

But that night, after Theon and Jolie had expired, I was paralyzed, unable even to imagine reading. Big Dick Palmer, completely without volition, had filled me with passion that Lana's sorrow had punctured and depleted. The deaths were a part of my paralysis but not essential to it, no more than Myron was a part of my orgasm. I felt closer to Lieutenant Mendelson's timidity and Lana's unabashed grief than I did to my own husband, his weakness and self-demolition.

Theon had abandoned me but men had been leaving me all my life. His death was a more familiar occurrence than all the years we spent together.

After failing to summon up the will to

reach for my book I tried to recall the feeling of my unexpected orgasm. I closed my eyes and imagined that spot of pain and Myron's grunting and Carmen Alia's clicking, insectlike camera. But none of it worked. I was numb, had been numb for years but never really knew it. I sometimes experienced this feeling of detachment as disinterest. At other times I mistook my lack of connection for the natural disdain a beautiful woman has for an ugly world. I had, for many years, taken for emotion the hungry look that men and women had for me. I had falsely perceived my own sensations as their oohs and aahs, grunts and groans, catcalls and blown kisses.

These ideas settled in my bed with Lana's breathing and the thought of Theon on a slab somewhere.

I remembered when Theon had proposed to me.

We were in a small casino in Vegas and both drunk. Theon got sloppy when he drank too much. Matching him drink for drink I moved, and thought, a little slower. The inebriation brought on by alcohol was just a more leisurely version of my sobriety.

"Let's get married," he said while fingering me under the table.

I was young, and wet, and Theon had driven us to Vegas in a fire-engine-red Rolls-Royce (which was leased but I didn't know that at the time).

"Okay," I said with a leer, "but no more PJ for you until there's a ring on my finger and we've both said 'I do.'"

I didn't think he was serious. I mean who would want to marry an eighteen-year-old girl who fucks for a living?

But Theon took me in a taxi to an aqua-and-pink-plaster twenty-four-hour chapel, where he presented me with a very expensive emerald and diamond engagement ring and paid a thousand dollars for the finest fast-food marital service.

What I remembered was the fact that he was thoughtful enough to have brought the ring on our little holiday, that and the smile on his face when I said the words of acceptance. I felt something then, like a smile drifting from my center up toward my lips.

Evoking that memory I tried to cry but couldn't. Even the best moment of my thirteen years of marriage with Theon failed to summon up a tear.

I lay there frozen and unfeeling, like a corpse in the snow waiting for the spring thaw. This sense of death brought an unexpected calm into my breast.

Theon was gone, running into death after the same quim he'd chased since the day he achieved his first erection. Jolie, I felt, somehow died in my place, enticing him with her passion to be seen and adored while collecting a paycheck and pining for love.

These plain truths soothed me. I shifted onto my side and lost consciousness while breathing in the sweet scent of Lana's troubled sleep.

Someone was kissing my left nipple. It was a feathery kiss with a small lick at the end. The kisser was experienced, knew how to keep their hunger at bay while physically expressing a rapacious desire.

"Hello," I said.

I opened my eyes on a sun-drenched morning. Lana was leaning over me, retreating from my big, black, wet nipple.

She blew on it and said, "I'm sorry, Deb, I just always wanted to do that."

"It's okay with me but what would Linda Love have to say?"

"You won't tell her, will you?"

"Of course not."

Hearing this, Lana closed her small mouth and breathed in through her nose, somehow communicating that she'd like to show me

25

other things she'd always wanted to do.

"Not today, baby," I said. "I just couldn't after all that happened."

"I understand," she said. And she did too. She understood that I would never be her lover but that I wasn't rejecting her as a person.

"Help me up?" I said.

Little Lana got on her knees and pulled my wrists. This movement imbued me with energy again. I remember feeling that if I had been alone I might have never gotten up.

"I'll go make us breakfast," she said.

When Lana left the room I went to the closet and was rendered immobile again for a time. There were latex minidresses, and cashmere pantsuits with holes stitched in so that I couldn't really wear underwear with them. I had a few Catholic-girl miniskirt uniforms and a dozen pairs of pants that fit so tight they adhered to my sex close enough that the casual stranger could know my form as well as Theon did. I'm naturally tall, so the rows of five-inch heels and platform shoes were designed to make me tower over most men. My blouses were all two sizes too small — T-shirts too. I couldn't sit without exposing myself in the little black dresses, and all of my panties were white and thong.

"Black-and-white is my signature," I often said, "from me and my Caucasian husband to this small black dress and my white silk panties."

I could hear Lana in the kitchen making our breakfast. This act, more than the kiss, told of the love she harbored for me.

At the back of the twenty-four-foot-wide, five-foot-deep closet was a brown paper bag that contained a calf-length yellow-and-blue dress that I filched from a BBW named Wanda in a specialty film I'd once made. Wanda weighed two hundred eighty-five pounds and that dress fit her like a glove. Under that was a pair of worn blue tennis shoes. Inside the left shoe was a .32 caliber midnight special, the only legacy my father had left after being shot in the street by a thug named Kirkland. He'd staggered into the house and into my mother's arms, blood spilling over her clean white dress and the floor.

As I was putting on the billowy dress the phone rang. I heard it but felt no need to answer. It rang five times before it stopped and Lana piped, "Hello?"

She talked intermittently. I could make out random words but not the sentences they formed.

I finished dressing, put my father's gift into a big blue purse, and headed for the kitchen.

I don't know why I decided to take my father's pistol; maybe my meditations on death resonated with the hardware the way Professor Abraham's books echoed through history.

On the way out I passed my full-length mirror. The dress served its purpose, so I didn't pay any attention from the neck down. What caught my eye was the head and face.

I've been told many times that I am beautiful. My father, a small-time hood, said it every day that he and I shared this earth. There was a temporary white-stain tattoo under my left eye. It was a perfect circle, two inches across with a dime-size white dot off-center inside. That was my signature. Even Theon didn't know it was a stain. He wanted to mark me, to deform me, but I never could go with that.

My straightened, bleached-white hair came down way past my shoulders. Sometime during the night I had taken out the deep-sea-blue contact lenses, so my eyes were their natural dark brown color.

I took a pair of chrome-plated scissors from the dresser and began to hack away at the hair that so many men had yanked on and women had caressed while penetrating my sex and rectum, slapping a black ass that would swell but never blush.

"I like your hair, Deb," Lana said when I finally made it to the kitchen. She was still naked.

"Really? I left most of it on the bedroom floor. You can hardly tell it from the white shag but I suppose you could pull it up with a vacuum cleaner."

"I mean I like it short, silly. It's so cool how uneven it is. You turned from Marilyn Monroe to punk-slut with just a few snips."

"Who was on the phone?" I asked.

"Richard Ness."

"What did that fool want?"

"Theon. I told him what happened and he hung up."

Just then the kettle began to whistle and Lana turned her attention to the French-press pots. She'd prepared them with the Italian roast coffee I loved.

There was low-fat turkey bacon sizzling on the grill and egg-white omelets cooking in their special Teflon pans. Lana gestured at the breakfast nook, which was nestled in between three mostly glass walls that looked out on Theon's pride and joy: a lawn of

Kentucky bluegrass.

He'd look forward to every late spring when the green grass bore its blue flowers.

"I love that grass as much as your ass," he used to tell me.

The memory of those words almost pierced the veil and brought Theon back from the dead, so much so I feared that my mind could conjure him and lose something that was waiting for the girl in the ugly dress and down-at-the-heels blue tennis shoes.

"I made a decision last night," Lana said, breaking through my fears.

"Oh? What's that?"

The breakfast had been served while I fought off the dead. I had juice and coffee, turkey bacon, a grilled slice of tomato, and an Egg Beaters omelet on an oblong plate.

"I know this is your moment, Deb," she said, "that you lost your husband and all. But when I saw him and that girl in the bathtub I realized how awful what we do is. It was like everything in there had a meaning. His half-hard dick and her draped over him like that — the camera in the water and the house all shorted out. I realized that I had to quit this business and break away from Linda."

"What would you do?" I asked. I really wanted to know.

"Get a straight job and maybe a boyfriend or something."

"Is Leer really your last name?"

"No. It's Koski. Kristin Koski. Linda gave me the name Lana Leer. She said that it sounded better and that you should never use your real name in the credits of a film."

"Were you ever on camera?"

"That's how I met Linda. She could tell how much I hated it and took me in."

"Why not go by your old name if you're not acting anymore?"

"I don't know," she said, letting her head loll to the side like Perry Mendelson had done the night before. "My parents kind of disowned me and I guess having a new name was me letting go of them. Is Dare your name?"

"Peel," I said. "Sandra Peel. I was born in Inglewood to Aldo and Asha. She was a seamstress for a Jewish tailor downtown and he was a thug but I loved him."

Lana smiled and then she laughed.

"What's funny?" I asked.

"I always like the way you talk, Deb. Most people . . . most people say one thing and then somebody else has to ask for more. You know, like if you said your real name was Sandy Peel and stopped there. But it's like you tell the whole story. Like you were

31

on a stage or somethin' and the rest of us were at the play."

Skinny little Lana was probably in her early thirties with short-short brown hair that showed a few gray sprouts here and there. Her big eyes were gray — almost white.

"What are you looking at, Deb?"

"Hmm?"

"You were staring."

"Oh. I'm sorry. I just wanted to see you. You know, my great-grandmother Henrietta used to say that people are always going so fast that they never appreciate where they are, who they're talking to."

"So you were appreciating me?" Lana asked behind a half smile.

The question didn't want answering. Lana was happy under my watchfulness and I was aware that something had come to an end, like a crescendo in a piece of classical music or at the conclusion of a scene in a play where the lights are still up and maybe even the actors are still onstage but there's no movement or speaking, only a pause before the next action. This, I thought in that brief moment, punctuated by Lana's half smile, was the beginning of the beginning after Theon's foolish end.

"Where the fuck are you, motherfucker?"

a man yelled.

We could hear him stomping in through the entrance room, into the wide hallway, and from there to the door of the kitchen.

Tall and broad, Richard Ness was both ugly and oddly attractive. He was a white man with darkish skin clad in a ridiculous light green suit. His nose had been broken so often that it looked like a pillow with the indentations of a night's sleep left on it.

I clutched my bright blue leather bag, the weight of my father's gun feeling like a premonition.

"Where the fuck is he, Deb?"

"What are you doing here, Dick?" I replied.

"Don't fuck with me, bitch."

"Never have, never will."

There was something soft about the thug Ness; you could see it in his eyes. My playful disdain for his manhood stung him. He was just a boy posturing the way boys think men are supposed to be.

"I'm lookin' for Theon."

"He's dead, Dick."

"Yeah, right."

"He was electrocuted in the bathtub with some girl he probably promised a job in my new movie."

Lana had both hands on the table, her

fingers curled into hardscrabble landbound bird claws. There was a tremor going through her.

"I will tear this house apart," Richard promised.

"He's down at Threadley Brothers Mortuary. The cops said it was a stupid accident. Why don't you call down there if you don't believe me?"

Lana's eyes were pleading with mine. I smiled at her. I really felt relieved; Dick's interruption was easier to deal with than my world turning upside down.

"Why don't you suck my dick?" Richard said.

"Dick's dick," I said lightly.

My calm caused him to clench his fists and scowl. He really didn't know what to do in the absence of fear.

"What would it cost you to call, Dick?" I asked. "I don't know what business Theon had with you, but I certainly wouldn't let you mess up my house if I knew where he was."

"You know something?" he said, his mouth puckering up like a baby's when it tastes its first lemon. "I always hated your cool bullshit. You think you're better than everybody, but I will kick your ass like Theon should have. I will make you crawl like a fucking worm."

Ness took two long steps forward.

Lana reached for a fork on the table.

I smiled at the futility and bravery of Lana's action and then pulled my father's chrome-plated midnight special from out of the blue bag.

Ness registered the weapon with his small eyes but took another step, more out of reflex than bravery.

I pulled back the hammer and it snapped loudly, like some bug warning a larger predator of its venom.

Ness stopped.

Lana began hiccuping.

"My husband is dead," I said. "And if you don't move your ass out of my house you can collect whatever it is he owes you in hell."

Lana hiccuped loudly and brought both hands to her mouth. In her left she still clutched the fork.

"Don't be crazy, bitch," Richard Ness said.

"What did you call me?" I said softly, dangerously.

Ness's hesitation humiliated him. The shiver that went through his battered face told of the man he wanted to be but wasn't. He wanted to come at me regardless of the pistol, rip the gun from my fingers, and batter me to the floor.

But he stayed in his place.

I stood up, luxuriating in my frumpy dress, and Richard fell half a step backward. He was looking in my eyes for some kind of weakness. His disappointment showed itself as a squint.

"I will kill you, Dick. Because you know, I'm not cool — I just don't give a fuck."

I had decided with those last six words to kill Richard. It felt right. The deadness, the orgasm, the death of the shallow-but-sweet man I called husband.

The muscle in my trigger finger contracted.

Richard leaned back, closing his left eye completely.

Lana hiccuped again.

"Hello? Anybody home?"

The voice came from the front of the house. It was male and sounded familiar but I couldn't place it right off.

"Back here!" I shouted, giving up on the murder I wanted so badly to commit.

Just before Lieutenant Mendelson walked into the kitchen I placed my gun hand into the purse while still holding on to it, because I didn't know if Richard was armed or what he might do if he had the chance to grab me.

"This is Perry Mendelson, Dick," I said. "He's the detective investigating Theon's death."

Richard's big broken face showed a great deal of relief. He knew from the look in my eye that he was very close to the terminus of his life. A few seconds earlier I was going to kill him and claim self-defense — now . . . I wasn't.

"Theon's really dead?" the thug asked.

"Yes, he is," Perry said, his senses filled with the unnamed danger that had just passed.

"Murdered?"

"It looks like an accident. I just came by to ask Mrs. Pinkney some questions about the woman he was with. Were you a friend of his, Mr. . . . ?"

"Ness. Richard Ness. I'm a . . . I was an associate of Mr. Pinkney."

"What kind of business did you do together?"

"Movie production . . ." Ness said, looking at me. ". . . that and financial advice."

"Would you happen to recognize this woman?" Perry took a photograph from the side pocket of his gray suit jacket.

"You really are a cop?" Richard said.

I noticed that the tension went out of the big man's burly, lime green shoulders.

"Policeman," Perry said correcting the term. "Lieutenant Mendelson. Do you recognize this woman?"

Richard took the photograph between two blunt fingers and examined it.

"I better go put on some clothes," Lana said.

Lana was unobtrusive sitting there, almost invisible. She had a prepubescent boy's body, with small breasts and a shaved pubis. When she darted out of the room Perry averted his eyes from an innate sense of propriety. Richard didn't look because he didn't care.

"No, Lieutenant," he said. "I've never seen this young woman before. Looks like jail-bait."

"And you, Mrs. Pinkney?" Perry said as he retrieved the photograph and held it up for me. "Do you remember your husband talking about this young woman? Or maybe you even met her at some point?"

Jolie was lying on a slab in the picture. Her black hair was pulled back to show her face.

I had seen her looking worse.

"No, I haven't," I said. "Would you stay and have a cup of coffee with Lana and me?"

The question was carefully phrased. I

wanted Perry to know that he was welcome while Richard was not. He caught the drift and turned his gaze on the leg breaker, loan shark, hustler, thief, and coward.

"Well, I guess I better be goin'," Richard mumbled. "You have my condolences, Debbie. You know, usually when I'm told that people who owe me money are dead I take it with a grain of salt."

There was a moment of absolute silence in that vast blue suburban kitchen. Then Richard nodded and walked swiftly from the room.

I followed, blue bag in hand, going all the way to the front door (which, I realized, the police must have left unlocked the night before) and watched the man who nearly died at the foot of my breakfast table get into his vintage purple Impala and drive off.

"Was he giving you trouble?" Perry asked at my back.

"No," I said, "not at all. Dick thinks that because he's so big and ugly that people are supposed to be scared of him, but not me."

I stood there looking out at the blue, blue July morning, Perry Mendelson behind me, peering over my shoulder.

"You cut your hair."

"I had to do something."

I felt him holding back from touching my

shoulder; I was sure of it. I wanted that touch. How long had it been since I yearned for a man's hand on me?

I turned to him and said, "Let's go get that coffee."

When we got back to the dining nook, Lana was there wearing her faded blue jeans and a pale violet T-shirt from my dresser drawer. When she saw Perry with me she got up and set another place at the table.

"You don't have to bother," Perry told her.

"Oh, that's okay," she said, displaying that crooked smile. "There's lots of room and food."

"Just coffee for me . . . black."

Lana's expression was mild and yet overflowing with feeling. Men filled two roles in her life: predators and fathers. Perry, at least momentarily, had taken up the daddy position in her quivering heart.

"We'd really like to get a line on this girl," Perry said when we settled across from each other. "She has a family somewhere, people who care about her."

"Didn't your people find her purse or anything?" I asked. "Wasn't there something in her pockets?"

"Forty-seven dollars and some makeup."

Poor Jolie. She didn't even have a pay-as-you-go cell phone. Girls like her slept in a different bed each week and washed out their panties by hand every night. Friends came and went one at a time, each one promising something and delivering somewhat less.

Theon had obviously offered her a career in adult films. Depending on how they met he might have asked me to help her out. He wouldn't necessarily have known that I'd already met the child.

Three weeks earlier my sometime producer, John Toland, had sent me to a hip-hop party at a music producer's home in Laurel Canyon. When I walked through the open front door I found myself in an audience of about thirty people. Everyone was black except for little naked white Jolie on her knees giving up-and-comer Fat Phil Harmonik a very energetic blow job.

The men in the room were mostly leering while the women sneered uncomfortably. I waited until the job was finished before taking Jolie by the hand and leading her around until we found a bathroom with a lock on the door.

I could tell by her eyes that she was only partly aware of where she was and what she was doing, so I laid her in the bathtub and turned on the cold water of the overhead shower. She was so high that it took five seconds or so for the chill to take effect. When she started shivering I held her in place for a few seconds more and then pulled her from the tub.

"Help me, miss," she said as I was drying her off.

"Do you know where you are?"

"No."

"Did somebody bring you here?"

"They must have but I don't remember."

Someone banged on the door.

"She's throwing up!" I yelled.

Then I took out my cell phone and hit a special code.

"Hello, beauty," he said on the second ring.

"I need help."

"Give me the address and I'll be there as soon as I swap out this passenger."

Forty-five minutes later I had the half-conscious child wrapped in a bathrobe. We were sneaking as best we could through the back of the house. From there we made it to a small gateway and down to the canyon road.

Short, dark, and unmistakably South American, the Brazilian Leonidas Asimante stood next to a black Lincoln Town Car waiting for us.

Once we were driving away I told him that I needed to take the girl (I had yet to learn her name) someplace where she could sober up.

"I have a client who keeps a house at the beach in Malibu," the flawless English-speaking driver said. "I look after it for him when he's out of town. You two can stay the night if you want."

I sat up with Jolie until the distant ocean glinted orange. She vomited bile and cried, thanked me over and over, told me her life story, and then fell so soundly asleep that she seemed dead, more so than in the photograph that Lieutenant Mendelson was showing me.

In the afternoon Leonidas came with clothes I had him buy. We dressed her and drove her to a rooming house I knew of down around Venice Beach.

"I have no idea who she is," I said, answering Perry Mendelson's query.

A look of concern creased the policeman's already doubtful visage.

Lana put a cup of black coffee down in front of the detective.

"What?" I asked.

"Excuse me," Lana said as she climbed over my lap to sit on the other side.

"It's just that I find it hard to believe," Perry said, "that a woman would have no idea how to at least find out what her husband is up to."

"You want Theon's cell phone?" I asked. "He never finished high school and didn't even know how to spell the word *computer*. But maybe there's a phone book in there somewhere."

"That won't help me if I don't know a name."

"You could just call every name until somebody doesn't answer," Lana offered.

"We don't have that kind of manpower," Perry said, taking her seriously. "I mean if this was a murder or something, but right now the worst is that it's an underage runaway that died."

"If she was underage like you say," I offered, "and she died having sex with a mature man like my husband . . . you could construe that as some kind of homicide."

"Yeah. Maybe second-degree manslaughter, I guess. But the chief of police and the city prosecutor wouldn't want to use public funds in that manner. You weren't here and so there's no living perpetrator."

44

"Can I be straight with you, Perry?" I asked.

"Sure."

"Do you recognize me?"

"Um . . . no. Not personally."

"Did some of the other cops last night make jokes?"

"Uh . . ."

"It's okay. I'm not shy. I take off my clothes in front of a camera and fuck for a living. That's the kind of business we're in — me and Lana . . . and Theon too, when he was alive. We've all met thousands of girls like the one from last night. With most of them I'm more likely to remember if their ass stank than their names.

"A dozen girls like that flutter around me every single day. To tell you the truth, Theon might not have known her name. And even if he did it wouldn't have been a real name. Nobody gives their real name — no, no, no."

He picked up on the reference to Fats Waller with a Lana-like smile and glanced down at his hands.

"You listen to Waller?" His words told more than they asked.

"My father loved old-time jazz. I used to sit on his lap and listen with him."

Our eyes met and I saw that he was experiencing hunger that was unfamiliar to him. He felt a connection with me and that made him uncomfortable.

"You like being a policeman?" I asked to relieve his tension and to explore it at the same time.

"I used to."

"Not anymore?"

"I still do the work," he said. "I think it's important but I care too much. A cop can't really care. We come across a dozen tragedies every day."

"I know what you mean."

"You do?"

"With me it's even worse. I have to pretend to care and I don't give a shit."

"I better be going," he said.

He stood up.

I nodded.

He turned.

I wanted to say something: the kind of words that held out hope for a next meeting.

He walked the distance to the kitchen doorway and I remained silent, telling myself that it wasn't the time and he wasn't the man.

"Deb!" Lana yelped maybe three minutes after Perry had gone. "We have to get to work. It's a ten-o'clock call."

"I thought you quit the business?"

"Uh . . . um . . . But Linda expects us."

"I thought you were breaking up with Linda?"

"I am but . . . but this is our job."

The bewildered look on her childlike face was perfect. Decisions and actions didn't have anything to do with each other in her mental life. She was a kid, from Ohio I think, who was still looking for the magic door that led to a place where things fit together because you wanted them to.

"Tell Linda I couldn't make it today," I said.

"She's gonna be mad."

"My husband died last night, honey. He was electrocuted in the bathtub where he was fucking an obviously underage girl. The police are questioning me. Richard Ness is on my ass. And in the meanwhile I have to bury Theon. You tell Linda that, and then, if she gets mad, you tell her to bring her skinny ass and her razor blade over here."

"O-okay, Deb. Don't be mad at me. I wasn't really thinking is all. Do you need a ride somewhere?"

"Back to my car?"

"It was parked on the street and so I gave Linda your keys. She said she'd have someone drop it off in the afternoon."

"That's okay then. I'll take Theon's Hummer."

"Do you want me to stay and help you?"

I could have said yes but that would have torn Lana apart. She had to go back to Linda and the set. She had to do what she was told because that was how she had survived all these years.

"No, baby," I said.

"What are you going to do?"

"What every girl does when she needs to think."

"Hairdresser?"

I smiled and she did too.

Half an hour after Lana had gone I went out to the driveway to ignite Theon's bright yellow Hummer. It was the largest model ever made and even a tall person needed the extra step to climb up into the driver's seat.

I grabbed onto the door handle and was about to pull myself up when he spoke.

"Hey, Deb."

I should have known that Richard wasn't the kind of dog to let a bone go so easily.

The pistol was in the house so I was on my own against the huge bundle of woman-hating violence. The fact that he was a coward only made him more dangerous.

"Hey, Dick."

"I don't like people callin' me that."

"That's okay, Dick. I don't like you." My heart was thundering and there was too much blood in my brain to make room for the underlying fear.

"I'm gonna kick your ass, bitch."

"I don't think so."

"No? Why not?"

"Two reasons," I said as if from the middle of a dead calm somewhere far out at sea. "First, if you take one more step I will holler bloody murder and you better believe every one of these housewives around here will call nine-one-one. Two — and you have to listen closely to this one, Dick — two is that if you don't kill me, I will get that gun and blow you away . . . today, tomorrow, sooner or later. So if you kill me you'll never get what Theon owed, and if you don't it won't matter."

His fists clenched and I took in a deep breath — ready to scream.

I was counting on the fact that Theon always said that Richard was an intelligent man in spite of his looks.

His hands unclenched and he took in a deep breath.

"He owes me seventy-two grand."

"Can you prove it?"

49

"He signed my book."

"You got it on you?"

"I could just take your key and drive your Humvee outta here."

"Then I'd call the cops and you can play Grand Theft Auto with the other fools in jail."

It was a dangerous game but Richard was forcing it. He wasn't the kind of guy who gave away anything — no real loan shark is. They always move straight ahead; that's why they called them sharks.

"I'll call you," he said.

"And we'll meet someplace public," I added. "Not here. If I see your ass here again I'll put a cap in it."

I should have gone back in the house and had some tea after Richard left for the second time. My body chemistry was way off and I needed to calm down. But the adrenaline in my blood wouldn't let me even try to relax.

On La Brea just south of Wilshire I tried to change lanes without putting on the blinker and smacked into a navy blue Saab. I pulled to the curb and waited. The young black man driving the Saab jerked his car up behind mine and leaped out. He walked around, assessing the damage to his car in a herky-jerky manner that would have been funny if I didn't know what had just happened.

I climbed over to the passenger's side and emerged slowly, perusing the damage to his car and mine.

"What the hell do you think you're doing?" he shouted.

There was good reason for his rage. My car barely had a scratch while his was pretty torn up. Theon had an ornamental pipe running along the side of his car. This garish accessory gouged a deep gash along the side of the Swedish-made car.

A young Asian girl, who was at least seven months pregnant, got out of the Saab. She waddled up next to the lanky driver, willing him, it seemed, to calm down.

"I was in the wrong," I said. "I'm very sorry."

"It was your fault!" he hollered.

"That's what she said, Willie," the girl murmured.

"Stay out of this, Tai."

"We should trade insurance numbers," I suggested.

Tai was staring at my face.

"What the hell are you gonna do about my car?" he replied.

"We can wait for the police to come if you want," I said calmly. I didn't want the police there. I never much liked being around cops.

"Willie," Tai said.

His eyes were bulging and a tremor was going through his thin frame.

"Willie," pregnant Tai said, some fear now in her voice.

I wondered if I should be afraid, if Willie was about to lose his mind and kill me right there on La Brea.

Then the young man fell to his knees.

"Help me," Tai cried. She went down too, grabbing Willie by his left arm.

"What's wrong with him?" I asked.

"Seizures," she said. "He has them sometimes when he gets upset."

I suspected that Tai was not from the United States, though she certainly spoke English well enough. Maybe she was from some ex–English colony somewhere. I say this because any good Angeleno would know that I could take the knowledge of his condition and use it against him in traffic court.

"We have to call an ambulance," she cried.

"Help put him in my car," I said, "and follow me."

I grabbed Willie's other arm and, with Tai's help, hefted him up into the seat. We strapped him in; then she ran to her car. I turned over the engine and said loudly, "Call Neelo Brown."

I pulled away from the curb followed by the tattered Saab.

The car's speakers engaged and then came the sound of ringing.

"Dr. Brown's office," a pleasant female voice said.

"Zelda?"

"Debbie?"

"I've got an emergency."

There was a pause on the line. There always was when I called Neelo's office. Zelda didn't dislike the syndicate of porn actresses that had sent her boss through medical school, but she was a medical professional and so she perceived us as a threat to his practice.

"Can you come in?" Zelda asked.

"I'm a mile or so away."

"I'll set the gate to your garage key."

"I'll be there soon."

I could see Tai in the rearview mirror. The fear in her face was apparent even from that distance.

There were flecks of white foam at the corner of Willie's mouth. He was shivering and barely conscious.

■ ■ ■ ■

Two wrongs, they say, cannot make a right, but if you put enough negatives in the pot there's a chance, I believe, that they might cancel one another out.

On the ride up to Sunset Boulevard, with the boy-man maybe dying next to me and the girl crying in the car behind, a familiar numbness entered my heart. I felt patient with the unfolding of events, treating them in my mind as the unavoidable consequences of a life of my own choosing.

My negativity pot was full to overflowing. There was a dead husband whom I loved but couldn't bring myself to grieve for, and a young girl, also dead, who wanted a life that would forever elude her; there was the leg breaker and the woman-child, Lana, who wanted to be loved for someone she hoped to be; there was the cop whom I admired and lied to and the hundreds of books I'd read but never understood; there was a boy named Edison who had a perfectly round head and a woman named Delilah who guarded him — even from me.

The list of ingredients was longer than that. I'd done many things wrong and known many people who were crooked but not bad, pretty but not beautiful, religious with no God, young to look at but never innocent.

Neelo's office was in a nondescript nine-story medical building just north of Sunset.

Approaching the gray-green metal door I pressed the remote control for our garage and the door magically slid open. Tai made it in before the door slid back into place. We drove thirty feet to a set of double doors that were already open.

Two big men in hospital white were waiting there with a wheelchair between them.

"What's the problem, Mrs. Pinkney?" one of the men asked. He was a tall and well-built man of Scandinavian descent.

"This kid has had some kind of seizure."

"What's going on?" Tai said, running up to us as well as she could in her condition.

"This is a clinic, ma'am," the other paramedic said. From his accent I could tell that he was African, probably Nigerian. "We're taking this man to the doctor."

Tai chose that moment to swoon.

The African ran to her and, with impressive ease, picked her up in the cradle of his arms.

"Come, miss," he said to me.

■ ■ ■ ■

The waiting room was small and anonymous. Tan walls, light green carpeting, and a low table with magazines like *Good Housekeeping* and *O.*

I felt completely safe. No one knew I was there. There were no cameras or oversize erections on muscular men in the next room waiting to rip off my clothes and fuck me from every angle, in every orifice; there were no gaffers or hot lights, smells of lubricants or alcohol.

I wanted to read a book about a place so far away that nobody in this world could get there. The story would be about a woman whose hair had turned white from age readying to bury her husband. There would be a problem — something about property and male lineage — but I'd be concerned only with wrapping his limbs tight to his body after washing him clean from a lifetime of honest but dirty labor.

"Aunt Deb?"

Neelo Brown was of medium height and always, since childhood, a little chubby. He was only five years younger than I but in his eyes I might as well have been his mother's age.

Neelo's mother, Violet Caracas, was a real porn star out of the eighties. She was one of the first to take her career into her own hands and had shown many of us girls how to do the same.

I was seventeen when I met her and Neelo; Theon had introduced us. Neelo was so good at his classes that he'd skipped three grades and was about to graduate from junior high school. I had a fake ID and was already making two thousand a week doing DP scenes for Reel Women Pictures in the Valley. Violet got a group of us together and introduced us to her accountant.

Thirty-six months later she was dying from pancreatic cancer and five of us girls promised to see that Neelo got through college.

After he graduated from medical school Neelo had his accountant set up a private insurance plan for girls in the business. The primary five got special treatment. We were all his aunts.

"Hey, baby," I said. "You're looking good."

I loved how he looked at me. It was the way a young man appreciated a favored relative.

"You cut your hair," he said.

"Theon died."

"Oh my God," he said from knee-jerk emotions that young men in the straight life are guided by. "What happened?"

"It was an accident. He electrocuted himself."

"When?"

"Last night or maybe yesterday afternoon. When I got home after nine the police were already there."

"What does Norman have to do with that?"

"Norman?"

"William Norman . . . the man you brought in."

"Oh. Willie. Nothing. I just ran into him and he had this fit. How is he?"

"I don't know. He responds to treatment like an epileptic would. I haven't tested him though. His wife is resting. I didn't want to give her any drugs because of the pregnancy but all I had to do was tell her that her husband would recover and put her in a dark room and she fell asleep."

He smiled. Neelo Brown smiled and my life shifted course, ever so slightly. A breeze blew into that dead calm and my path had changed continents. I didn't know it at the time. I was still thinking about Theon and Jolie, Big Dick Palmer and the first orgasm I'd had in a decade.

"What, Aunt Deb?"

"Huh?"

"You're smiling."

"Can you look after the kids, Neely? I really have to be somewhere."

"No problem."

"If Willie wants my number give it to him. I slammed into his car so I guess this seizure is my fault. Put it on my bill?"

"What bill? You know your money's no good here, Aunt Deb."

Rhonda's Beauty Salon was on Pico a few blocks east of Hauser. Rhonda was petite and mannish, black haired and blue eyed, tender and giggly — she was a white woman raised among black people, a ninety-pound weakling who never went anywhere without a razor somewhere close at hand.

"Hey, baby," she said as I walked into the open door of the storefront business.

There were three young black hairdressers, two women and one man, working on clients along the east wall. Rhonda was in back sitting in her pink leather beauty chair. She lowered a copy of *Jet* magazine to greet me.

"Hi, Rhonda," I said softly. "You got time for me?"

"I always got time for my movie star," she

said, dropping the tiny magazine in a pouch at the side of the chair. "What you need?"

"Darken my hair and give it some body. And take this white circle off my cheek."

"Uh," she grunted. "Baby girl is quittin' the industry."

As I took the seat I thought about Lana telling me that she was through with the business, and the hair on the floor of my bedroom, about an imagined picture of Richard Ness lying at my feet leaking blood onto the kitchen floor through a hole in his eye socket.

". . . yeah," Rhonda was saying as I thought about a future I could not exactly imagine. "Derek is a no-good lazy niggah but he love my skinny li'l white ass like it was the first peach in season."

"What's he doin' now?"

"Nasty young ho named Cassie done messed up my sheets, *my sheets,* with Derek's stuff an' then sit her stank ass in this here chair askin' for the cut rate. You know I did her whole head an' then I put a razor to her neck an' whispered in her ear that if I evah saw her again I was gonna cut that pretty black th'oat from one side all the way to the othah." Then she let out a deep, sinister chuckle. "You know Miss Cassie

Ass-Worth done left the neighborhood since then."

"I'm surprised you didn't cut off Derek's thing," I said.

"I would if I didn't like the way he work it so good. You know, Deb, I ain't nevah had a man love me like he do. He know every touch on my body and every word in my head."

I could almost experience the thrumming passion in Rhonda's body as she leaned close to massage my scalp. It was as if her emotion was water or air passing over me. I took a deep breath and closed my eyes.

"What's happenin' with you, girl?" Rhonda asked after the tide of her emotions ebbed a bit. "How come you quittin'?"

"Theon's dead."

"What?"

Rhonda levered the chair up from its reclining position and twirled me around until I was facing her.

"He what?"

I told her most of the story, everything except the part about me knowing Jolie.

"Oh my God," Rhonda said when I'd finished. "Well . . . I guess they got what they deserved."

"Nobody deserves to die when they have a chance at life," I said.

"So you forgive Theon like I did Derek?"

"I fuck for a living, Rhon. You know the best thing Theon could do for me after a hard day was make me some chamomile tea and rub between my toe bones."

Hearing this Rhonda took on an expression of confusion wrapped in pity.

My hair was dark brown and wavy and the tattoo was almost completely gone. Rhonda explained that the dyes used over the years to maintain the white circle and disk had stained the skin and that it would take a while for the pale shadow to recede.

On my way to the accounting offices of Mintoff and Myers I called a number that Theon's car phone knew by heart.

"Threadley Brothers Mortuary," a woman said with liveliness you wouldn't expect from an undertaker.

"Hi, I'm calling about Theon Pinkney. This is his wife."

"Oh yes. We have the remains and were wondering what to do."

"I want to come in around six to make the arrangements. Will Lewis be there?"

"Yes, Mrs. Pinkney," the woman said. Even though I'd never gone by the name Pinkney, I liked the anonymity of its usage. It was as if I were somebody else — hiding in plain sight.

I drove straight down Pico toward the ocean. When I got to Lincoln I turned left and went for about a mile or so. On the way no one tooted their horns or made lewd gestures as was often the case. My look had been so unique and pornography was so widely viewed that I was more recognizable than most movie stars. Men (and women) asked for my autograph, honked their horns, and offered me money to show my breasts — I didn't always refuse them.

Chas Mintoff and Darla Myers's office was on the second floor of a shabby building three blocks up from the beach. They were both surfers and musicians. Sometimes they were lovers. Now and again I joined them. But our only real connection was that they were honest accountants who took care of our investments.

"Hey, Deb," Juana Juarez, the receptionist, greeted. "I almost didn't recognize you."

Juana was the color of amber, freckled, and afflicted with a smile that would not be dominated. If she knew about my work she refused to comment on it. If I ever needed a friend she would have been the person I would have chosen.

"Are they in?" I asked.

Juana pushed a button on the big blue office phone.

"Yes, Juana?" a woman said.

"It's Debbie for you guys."

"Send her in."

Their desks were positioned across the room from each other, slanted away so that where they'd meet (if you continued the lines) they would form a perfect right angle. This seemed appropriate; they led away from and toward each other at the same time.

"Hey, Deb," blond-haired, green-eyed Chas said.

"Hi," his counterpart, the mousy brunette Darla, murmured.

Whenever approaching the partners you were faced with a choice: sitting next to one desk or the other. This wasn't odd seeing that they rarely represented the same client.

Theon and I were one of the few exceptions.

"You cut your hair," Chas noticed.

"And had your tattoo removed," Darla added.

"Theon got electrocuted in the bathtub with some teenage girl. They were trying to make a movie but the camera fell in."

The accountants stood in unison and moved toward me, Chas pulling his chair and the guest seat and Darla rolling her own, specially made, wicker office chair.

"I can't believe it," Chas mumbled.

"Sit down," Darla said.

I went over the details I cared to share. Big Dick Palmer didn't make the cut; neither did the name Jolie. I went into detail about Richard Ness and his seventy-two-thousand-dollar request.

"But, baby, you guys are in hock up over the line," Darla told me. "You know that, don't you? You signed all the documents."

"Sign the papers on the kitchen table, will ya, babe?" How many times had Theon said that to me? I hated legal mumbo jumbo, so I rarely read, and never understood, what I was signing.

"There's nothing left?"

Darla squinted while Chas looked down at his feet and hands. There was no sense in me blaming them. There was no comfort to be found in recriminations or rage.

"What about the Hummer?" I asked.

"If you don't pay fifteen hundred dollars a month the bank will take it away," Darla said softly.

"Where did all the money go?"

"I don't know what all he spent it on," Chas added, "but he was funding some pre-production expenses for a movie with Johnny Preston."

"A legit?"

"I think so. We've been in contact with Preston's business office."

"Any money on the horizon?"

"Not yet."

The youngish surfers each took one of my hands.

I held on tight. I don't think I would have ever let go except I had a funeral to plan.

I looked at my watch before getting out of the Hummer. It was five fifty-eight. I was almost always on time to any meeting or appointment. It's not that I looked at the clock or anything; it was more of an internal timepiece that ran like a little motor in the center of my being.

"Hello, Mrs. Pinkney," Lewis Dardanelle said when I walked through the front door of Threadley Brothers Mortuary.

The entrance hall was large, pretending to be vast. The floors and walls, even the ceiling, were tiled with varying shades of gray and green marble. The only furniture was a unique stone desk that the undertaker sat behind.

"Hey, Lew," I said.

He was up on his feet before I crossed the bleak expanse to the granite table. He gestured at an aluminum chair with a dull finish and I sat as demurely as the occasion required.

"I'm very sorry, Deb," he said. "Theon was so full of life."

"He was. Thank you."

"It was so unexpected."

Dardanelle was created to be a mortician; nearly six-six, he didn't weigh a pound over one sixty. His skin was pale, head bald, with rectangular glasses that were both thick and wide. Lew's fingers would have made great albino daddy longlegs; when they moved they seemed to have lives of their own.

He sat down, lacing the lanky digits of his hands.

"What shall we do?" he asked.

Theon and I had spent an inordinate amount of time and money at Threadley's. People died in our business with frightening regularity. STDs and cancers, some murders and a nauseating number of suicides, drug overdoses, and the odd death that even the county coroner couldn't explain — people who died in their rented houses, apartments, and trailers simply by exhaling and leaving this world behind.

We had paid out of pocket and chipped in with friends for many funerals: longtime acquaintances and one-night stands and ex-lovers who didn't have family. If I still had the money we'd spent at Threadley's I could have retired and moved to Wyoming, where the cost of living would have fit my purse.

"I'm broke, Lew," I said. "No stocks, no bonds, no cash, no property. Theon wasted it all. Or maybe he stole it — I don't really know."

Lewis's gray eyes were magnified and elongated by his lenses. They widened further to take in my words.

I'd spent a week with him when we planned the funeral of Oceanna Patel, who knew men so well that she could make them ejaculate without touching their genitals — on camera.

That funeral cost eighteen thousand dollars.

Death wasn't cheap and the funeral director met with would-be charity cases every day. Poor sad widows and confused children, brokenhearted lovers . . . they all came to him asking for a deal.

"There are certain rules," I once heard Dardanelle say to a sad, fat, fifty-year-old woman whose husband had killed himself. "We cannot make monetary exceptions. The city has resources for people in your circumstance."

I wasn't expecting Lew to help me but I had to ask — not for Theon but for myself. Nothing turns to dust faster than a dead sex worker. When I died no one would lift a finger to lay me to rest. At least I could try.

"You know the Threadley brothers have made it a rule that we have no economic flexibility."

"I know that."

"But we . . ." Lewis Dardanelle said and then paused. He frowned and then, quite uncharacteristically, smiled. "We have the names and contact information for people that you invited to other funerals."

"The guest lists," I said.

"I could have Talia call them and ask if they would donate something to the services."

"It could be a graveside ceremony," I offered. "We don't need a chapel."

"I'll call Talia at home and get her to start calling tonight."

"Why, Lewis? Why would you go out of your way like this?"

"Theon was always generous with the staff. He was a friend to me in many ways and I believe that I would be judged badly if I didn't help him on his way."

I don't know why I was surprised that an undertaker believed in an afterlife.

I ate dinner at a small French bistro called Monarc's a block north of Pico on Robertson. It was a simple meal of green beans and almonds with chicken cooked in a white-wine sauce. For dessert I had flan with raspberries and peach tea.

I read a few pages from a book I'd been carrying around in my big blue purse — *Behold the Man* by Michael Moorcock. It was a story of time travel and a kind of alternate Christianity.

"Excuse me, miss," a man said.

He was young and unremarkably dressed in business work clothes — California style: a herringbone jacket and light gray trousers, no tie but crystal cuff links on his white shirt. He was sitting at the table next to me reading a newspaper.

"Yes?"

"I see that you're reading science fiction," he said, smiling.

"Yeah . . . I guess. So?"

"Not so many single young women can be found eating alone and reading Moorcock."

"I'm not looking for company."

"Obviously not."

He was of mixed race, black and some kind of Caucasian or other light-skinned group. There was a gap between his front teeth and something like a question in his eye.

"Why obviously?" I asked.

"The fact of you sitting there like that, like I said before."

The way he talked was playful. I couldn't remember the last time someone played with conversation — with me.

"My name's Rash," he said. "Don't ask me why."

He held out a hand and I shook it against my better judgment.

"Sandra. Sandra Pinkney."

"Vineland is my family name."

"You don't know why your parents named you Rash, Mr. Vineland?"

"My dad always said that it just seemed right. My sister's named Susan and the younger brother is John."

"They must hate you," I said, feeling the smile take over my suspicions.

"Why do you say that?"

"Here your siblings were given vanilla names and you got something special, a name that one out of ten million don't get. You might be the only Rash Vineland in the whole world. I bet you are."

He squinted at my explanation and I liked him . . . some.

"You know," he said, "you might be right about that. I have to call John three times before he'll call me back, and Susan had a birthday party and invited everyone in the family except me. She said that the invitation must have gotten lost in the mail. But the way she said it made me wonder."

"You see?" I said, realizing that somehow Rash Vineland had lured me into conversation.

"Are you a therapist?" he asked.

"What do you mean?" The word had many connotations in my line of work.

"You know . . . a psychoanalyst or something like that."

I grinned. That might not seem like much but it was rare for me to express any kind of goofy humor. I'd pretty much stopped thinking that silly moments were worth laughing about on the day my father died.

"Why is that funny?" Rash asked.

"How old are you?"

"Thirty-two."

"And what are you doing here?"

"I like this place. I come here to read *The New York Times* at least twice a week."

"We're in Los Angeles."

"I know," he said, looking down at my worn blue tennis shoes. "It's kinda egotistical, I guess, something like that. I feel important reading the New York paper."

"Are your parents from there?"

"No."

"Have you ever been there?"

"Naw. Have you?"

"A few times."

"On business?"

"I have to go."

"To New York?"

"No. I have to leave . . . here."

There was no artifice to the disappointment in his expression. Rash wasn't going to ask me to stay or even if he could talk to me again. I imagined that he would come to Monarc's almost every day for a couple of weeks hoping to see me again. . . . Me, dressed in a pale-yellow-and-faded-blue muumuu with tattered tennis shoes on my feet.

I was liking him more.

"I'll tell you what, Rash."

"What?"

"I want you to write down your phone number on my place mat. I have no idea if I'll call you but at least I'll know how. Okay?"

"Absolutely."

■ ■ ■ ■

When I got home I turned on our state-of-the-art security system, retrieved my father's pistol, and made sure that it was loaded.

I changed the bullets yearly so that they'd have pop. My daddy taught me how to shoot on a range east of Riverside.

The answering machine had twenty-seven messages on it but I didn't listen to any of them. Instead I strolled through the dark house into the master's bedroom (as Theon always called it) and rolled up into the blankets thinking of a worm luxuriating in its own silk.

I turned on a lamp and started reading *The Autumn of the Patriarch.* That was a book I read often because it made poetry out of the rot and disarray of a life that seemed a lot like mine. The president was Theon and I was an unremarkable peasant among the hundreds who sometimes lived in his sphere. With these ephemeral ideas in mind I nodded and soon found myself asleep.

I loved Theon in my sleep that night. He was an ideal husband, a man who took care of so many people and things that he didn't have time for children — or even a proper job.

He broiled me steaks while preparing avocado salsas, squeezed lemonade from the fruit off our own tree, and then, after the meal, he washed the dishes before asking could he fuck my ass.

The sour lemonade on my dreaming lips ushered me into another dream:

I was on a posh set that I had once shot on in southern France. It was the living room that led to an outside veranda of some duke's mansion on the Mediterranean. There were four cameramen (not including photographers) and some of the most beautiful men I had ever seen. They were all naked and fully erect, looking at me haughtily and yet somehow hungrily.

"All right, Deb," Linda Love shouted.

I knew even in the dream that she didn't belong there. The director at the beach house was Polish, very tall, and dripping with the veneer of sophistication.

I looked in a full-length mirror that had been placed on the set and saw myself. My hair was long and white. The tattoo was there under my left eye. I could tell some-how that it was now permanent and a sad-ness filled me. My breasts were small again, sagging a little.

"Debbie."

"Yes, Linda?"

"This is going to be a revolutionary shoot. We're going to make millions on it."

"We?"

"The owners."

Then there was a tall beautiful man with tanned skin and no pubic hair standing before me. I fell to my knees and took the head of his huge, upstanding erection in my mouth.

"Slower, Deb," Linda whispered from across the room.

I could hear the waves crashing because the doors to the veranda were open wide.

"Slower?" I asked. All Linda had ever asked me for was more passion.

"You're making love to him," she said.

"What shot are you trying to get?"

"Don't worry about the shot. Just go with your feelings."

Whatever he did to me I wanted him to do. The feeling inside me was the sound of waves: waves in my womb, flushing out my rectum, across my clitoris, and rushing between my toes. I screamed with pleasure but the sounds were drowned by the turbulent Mediterranean Sea.

"I'm going to enter into your side now," my well-oiled lover said.

The room had grown to infinite proportions. The cameramen had put down their

cameras. Linda was reclining in her director's chair. The crew members were all sitting on the floor smiling and watching.

"You're going to turn me on my side?" I
asked.

"No," he said. He had a slight accent but
I couldn't place it. "I'm going to press my
cock in through your skin and under your
ribs, into your body."

"But that would kill me."

"You can learn to live with anything."

I wanted to say no but the scene of the
dream shifted and I was on a hassock with
the Adonis there next to me moving his
erection deeper and deeper into my side. It
was a very uncomfortable feeling, like gas
and freefall at once.

"See?" he said. "You feel it inside. They
all are watching me fuck you. They want to
see it from every side and in every way. You
feel me between your intestines, under your
heart, pressing, pressing?"

And for the briefest moment I tried; I
tried to accept his presence inside my body,
a sexual surgeon on a syndicated reality TV
program. I could feel the hunger and fear of
the crew as he pushed farther into me.

Then I woke up.

Actually I threw myself from the bed,
landing hard on the side of my left knee. I

was up immediately, fleeing from the bedroom. I turned on lights as I ran. I choked on a sour taste that seemed to rise up from my defiled internal organs. I made it all the way to our white-on-white sunken living room.

Theon had called it my polar bear room.

I had my father's midnight special in my hand.

The nacre clock on the wall was seven small white shells from midnight.

My sex was dry and shriveled like a very old woman's. The fear thrummed under my heart and I was shivering. I couldn't shake the images of the dream. They wanted to rip me wide open and expose my beating heart to excite some country fool's four-inch erection.

The phone rang at that moment. It seemed like fate.

I didn't move and the answering machine picked it up after the sixth burp of chimes.

"Sandra," a woman's voice said. "This is Dr. Karin. I read about your husband's death online and I wanted to call. Are you all right? If you want to see me I'm free all tomorrow afternoon. You can just drop by."

I wanted to pick up the phone but there was a pistol in my hand. I couldn't let the gun go, not at that moment. I couldn't.

There was a hesitation and then the click of Dr. Karin hanging up. I was relieved at her absence, overwhelmed with relief to be free from the dream. I also was ashamed of myself.

"Hold it open," the demented little director, who called himself DeLester Grind, had said to me after Myron had suddenly pulled his big dick out of my ass on my first anal shoot. "People want to see inside you. They want to imagine where that thing was."

"It's just a job," I told my mother that very afternoon. "They pay me and I pay your rent."

I believed those words. My poor black widowed mother needed somebody to look after her, just like a million men wanted to stare down my stretched and reddened rectum in order to sleep alone, or next to their wives — or both.

I stayed in the house all the next day with the phone turned off. Nobody rang the doorbell. I didn't even look outside. I didn't play music, watch TV, read a book or newspaper, or turn on the radio. I would sit in a white chair in the white room for hours staring at the white walls, wondering what my memories meant. Was it me, the woman alone in the house, who had starred in two hundred feature-length films that centered on my breasts and clitoris, my fake blue eyes — all dubbed in sighs?

My pale blue Jag had been returned to the driveway sometime during the day. After sunset I got in and drove with the sunroof open and all the windows down. When I made it out to the desert the air turned cold but I didn't mind.

I knew where I was going though I had never been there. It was a little house with a fruitless and perpetually dying apple tree in the front yard. There was a Beware of Dog sign on the chain-link fence but the ragged mutt was too old even to bark.

There were three cars parked on the lawn of the house. Actually it was a trailer with add-ons constructed on both sides and behind. Eerie lights blossomed from within. More than anything the structure resembled a cluster of luminescent mushrooms.

I walked up to the door wearing the yellow-and-blue muumuu, carrying the blue purse with my father's gun inside.

The front door was aluminum, corroded in spots. I knocked and then waited for no more than sixty seconds. A weak light came on over my head.

After a moment a frail woman's voice

asked, "Who's out there?"

"Mrs. May?"

"Who are you?"

"I'm Sandra Peel, ma'am. I came to bring you news about Myrtle."

"What news?"

"May I come in?"

"Are you alone?"

"Yes, ma'am."

"Do you know what time it is?"

"It's important."

"I don't know," the timid voice complained. "I don't know."

"I'll leave if you want me to."

"You could come back tomorrow," she suggested.

"I live pretty far away, Mrs. May. I might not be coming back."

It felt that the woman and I were merely giving voice to a bad script, a drama that we were acting in but had no part in writing, no heart in performing.

The door came open and a short and wide white woman stepped out onto the gray step. She was wearing a green robe over a T-shirt and jeans.

"What about Myrtle?" she asked.

"Can I come in?"

The front door opened into a wide and shallow living room. There was a TV tuned to a late-night repeat of *The Tonight Show* and a man, older than the woman, propped up in a wheelchair. He was held in place by a seat belt that crossed his chest from left to right.

The room smelled of stale urine and uninspired cooking. This atmosphere was sickening but I'd come too far to turn back.

"Only seat is on the couch, Miss Peel," the forty-something Mrs. May said. "I'll have to sit next to you."

The man let his head fall to the side so that he could see me with his watery russet eyes.

"Lester," Mrs. May said. "This is Sandy Peel. She's a friend of our Myrtle."

That room was why I'd fucked ten thousand men and women on four continents. Thousands of us boys and girls had run screaming from the same filth and stink of poverty. Black and white and brown and yellow and red had put out their thumbs and pulled down their pants, used lubricants and drugs and alcohol to escape these decaying ancestors and others just like them.

"Lester had a stroke six months ago," Mrs. May said. "I think it was because he was so heartbroken over Myrtle runnin' away."

"It killed her," I thought and also said out loud.

"What?" the broad woman asked.

"Myrtle's dead," I said. "She changed her name to Jolie Wins and came to L.A. to be a movie star. A producer offered her a job but there was an accident during the audition and she died from an electrical shock."

Lester had raised his head maybe half an inch.

"Dead?" Mrs. May said. "You come in here in the middle'a the night an' tell me my little girl is dead?"

"Yes, ma'am. You can call a Lieutenant Perry Mendelson of the Pasadena Police Department to get more exact information."

"Myrtle's dead," the woman said to Lester.

"And in a drawer in the Pasadena morgue."

"Why are you so cold?" Mrs. May's voice and Lester May's eyes asked me.

"Because I can't sleep, and even though you never knew enough to know that Myrtle hadn't been inside a classroom since she was twelve, you are her parents and you should know that she's gone.

"Because she told me where you lived and I have to believe that she wanted me to come here and tell you that she died trying to get as far away from you as she could. I believe that she wanted me to come here and ask Lester why he did what he did to her and to ask you why you closed your eyes and ears to her pain."

"You black bitch," Mrs. May said, her placid features turning into those of an ogre.

"Yes, ma'am," I said, "and much, much worse than that. Bitch and cunt and whore like you wouldn't believe. Yes, ma'am. Jolie sent a demon to announce her death. Now you can do what you want."

I stood up and Lester's eyes followed me. There was pity in that gaze but not, I think, for his daughter. He was feeling sorry for himself, for his loss, for his stroke. He was grieved that he was paralyzed in that room with a woman who transformed into a monster now and again.

I had brought my father's pistol maybe to kill them. If Jolie had been my daughter I would have sent her to school with Neelo Brown; I would have tried to love her.

As I drove away from the mutated trailer I told myself that the only reason I left Lester alive was so that he could suffer a little more, so that Mrs. May could keep him breathing while she collected his Social Security checks and boiled potatoes and guzzled beer until they both ran down the drain and into the sewer.

I woke up with the sun in my eyes. I had driven out to a fairly deserted campsite at Joshua Tree National Monument and slept there in the driver's seat of my pale blue Jaguar.

The moment I awoke I used the key to open the glove compartment and check out the ownership papers of my car. It was still mine, probably the only thing I owned. Somewhere Linda Love was looking for me and Richard Ness too. The sun was just risen and the desert held the chill from the night before. I got out of my car and went to the corrugated tin-walled camp outhouse.

A mother and father with three preadolescent boys were standing there. The boys had the jitters in their legs.

"Let the lady go first," the youngish blond woman said when an older gentleman, dressed in army surplus, came out of the crude toilet.

"That's okay," I said. "Boys feel the urgency more than women."

The father was staring at me. I was familiar to him but he couldn't place my face. This wasn't unusual. The odd thing about porno is that the face was usually the least memorable part of the experience. That's why I had a false tattoo and platinum hair. Those white marks against black skin made me stand out. Maybe the father just thought that a black woman in a pale *schmatta* was an odd visitor for a desert campsite.

"Here with your family?" he asked me as the boys crammed into the outhouse, slamming the tin door behind them.

"No. I used to come out here with my father when I was a kid. We'd make canned chili in a tin pot on a pit fire and pour it over a paper plate lined with Fritos. I was out this way last night and figured that it would be nice to sleep under a million stars and remember my dad."

"Not as many stars as there used to be," the man said with only mild lament. "Now civilization is closing in and the stars are fading."

He was an ugly man with friendly features: thin and Caucasian-brown with big dingy teeth and patchy hair sprouting from his chin. I had done a guy like that in a porno art film called *Amateur Nights,* made at a deserted gas station in Twentynine Palms — not that far from where we stood.

The pale-skinned wife was chubby and very pretty. She had the unconsciously haggard look of a feminine woman who lived in a house of maleness. She survived in an atmosphere of shouting, stomping boys and a man who cared but didn't really understand.

The door to the outhouse banged open and the brood of boys tumbled out, not quite zipped up or tucked in.

"I'm Sadie," the woman said to me. She held out a hand.

"Sandy," I said as we shook.

"You can go in now. Albert and I have already gone."

The aluminum toilet seat was wet because the boys hadn't put it up. They just pulled down their pants and had swordfights into the hole — getting their piss everywhere.

I used the stiff toilet paper to dry everything and then did my business. The mess and turmoil didn't bother me. I liked boys — always had. I liked their grins and hopes for triumph in battle. They made me laugh.

At the center of the camp was a huge pile of red boulders that might properly have been called a small hill. There were ridges and natural footholds that led up so you could climb the full thirty feet to reach the top.

I did this.

The west side of the stone hill was flanked

by an eight-foot-high, twenty-foot-long stand of spiky cholla cactus. The yellowy white needles numbered in the tens of thousands and some were as much as six inches long. There was a breeze at the top of the stone hill and you could see across the desert for miles.

It was my living limbo: the place that stood between an old life that had withered and died and a new one that had no form as yet. There was nothing I'd miss from the days I'd spent with Theon and, so far, nothing I could look forward to.

The children laughed, screamed, and sometimes cried across the camping area while the mother and father used stern voices to try to rein them in. The sun burned down on me like the memory of a thousand fuck scenes under intense electric light.

I got weak and dizzy up there but refused to come down. As long as I was on that red rock hill no one, except the little family, would know where I was.

"Excuse me, miss," the oldest of the three boys said.

He had climbed up into my little retreat.

"Yeah?"

"My mom said that you might be thirsty up here and she wanted me to bring you some water."

He held out an ice-cold eight-ounce bottle of water. I drank it in one steady gulp.

"That was good," I said.

"You were real thirsty," the dusty boy said in wonder. "My parents said that you could come to eat breakfast with us if you wanted to. It's really more like lunch but we call it breakfast because it's still morning."

His blue-green eyes were filled with innocent desire. It reminded me of something. I couldn't quite remember what.

"Darryl's in love," Errol, the second-oldest boy, sang.

We were all sitting together at the wooden picnic bench next to the family's campsite. White bread with bologna and mayonnaise was the entrée alongside watermelon on ice in a big Styrofoam cooler and Kool-Aid mixed up in a three-gallon jug with a spout at the bottom.

"You leave Darryl alone, Buster," Albert Freemont told the middle son. He rubbed Darryl's head and the boy both scowled and grinned.

"You look so familiar, Miss Peel," Albert said.

"I live in Pasadena. Do you spend any time there?"

"No. We're from Bellflower."

I shrugged and stood up. I hadn't had sex with anyone in more than forty-eight hours and it felt good — really good.

"Where you goin'?" Darryl asked.

"Darryl," Sadie said.

"What?"

"You shouldn't be so nosy."

"That's okay." I squatted down and kissed the ten-year-old on his cheek while both brothers oohed. "I just have to get back to my life."

"Will I see you again?"

"In this life you never know."

I was exhausted by the time I got home. It was late afternoon and I barely had the strength to stagger through the front door and turn on the alarm system. I made it to the twelve-foot, white cotton-covered couch in the polar bear living room. There I stretched out with the pistol next to my head. Sleep came down on me like a limp corpse.

My rest was a dead thing too: an unprotected body under a ton of soil backhoed in more to hide the stench than to protect the deceased.

The color of the darkness was not black. It was a mottled and opaque gray, revealing nothing but its formless self.

The ringing phone broke through the gray from time to time, and bodiless voices spoke out. I didn't recognize them; I didn't care. Light sometimes pressed in from the bleak landscape behind my closed eyes. Jets passed over me. Men took turns urinating on the grave above. I moaned out loud and prayed in a language unknown to me (and maybe to everyone else). I felt pains in different parts of my body, which, at rare intervals, forced me to shift position.

In that sleep I realized that death was an impermanent situation, a transition from bubbling thought to inert thing. The grave was also ever-changing but at a much slower rate. The ground was like glass — liquid but seemingly solid, flowing and yet so slowly that it would take centuries to move appreciably. And the thing that was my remains would flow with it, no longer rotting or stinking, writhing under ten thousand men, their eyes closed and dreaming of women who had unknowingly betrayed them.

The phone made its chimes at irregular intervals. The voices of men and women nattered at me. The doorbell rang but I slept on. The sun rose and set, rose and set. I remember staggering through the darkness to the toilet, twice. Somewhere Theon lay dead, his flesh slowly collapsing toward the earth.

Then there was somebody screaming loudly, beseechingly. Maybe there was a fire and a lost child, an explosion on a street somewhere named after a person I didn't know or in a language I didn't speak.

I was forced up out of the coffin of sleep, grasping my father's pistol.

The alarm system was blaring. Lights were going on and off all over the house. It was day, maybe morning, maybe afternoon.

Whatever door or window the voice says, you go in the opposite direction, Theon had told me when the sophisticated system was installed. He had been worried about men like Richard Ness coming after him in his sleep. He was still my husband, still taking care of me in his wrongheaded way, still alive.

The phone began to ring. That was the security company calling.

"Back door intruder," the recorded voice was saying over and over.

Whatever door or window the voice says, you go in the opposite direction.

I headed for the back door.

With an arm jutting through the broken window the intruder was just undoing the lock as I made it to the kitchen.

"Back door intruder!" the recorded voice spoke.

The telephone was ringing.

I was still at least half-asleep.

"Stop!" A single warning before I allowed myself to pull the trigger.

"Police!" a man's voice responded. It was simultaneously a plea and a command.

Perry Mendelson, the upper half of his light brown suit coming through my shattered back-door window, held up his hands to ward off bullets and suspicions.

"It's us, hon," Lana Leer screeched from somewhere behind him. "We thought you were dead, baby."

I was holding the gun so that Perry was looking down the barrel. He was scared. That made me smile. I lowered the pistol and went to the wall panel to disengage the alarm. Then I answered the ringing wall phone.

The security company had a special ring that bypassed the answering machine, so it would have rung all day.

"Everything's all right," I said into the receiver.

"Mrs. Pinkney?"

"Yes."

"What is the code phrase, please, ma'am?"

"Brer Rabbit."

"And what are the last four digits of your social?"

"Two, two, two, nine."

"And your maiden name?"

"Peel."

"Is everything all right?"

"My friends thought I was dead and they broke the backdoor window."

"Do you need help?"

"No."

"Are you sure?"

"I told you I'm fine and I answered your questions. Now I need to go look after my window."

"I'm sorry, ma'am, but it took you so long to get to the phone," the male security operator said. "One more minute and I would have had to call the police."

Perry and Lana had come into the kitchen. She was looking worried while he seemed embarrassed.

"I was dead asleep," I said. "I guess I've been depressed or something. It took me a while to realize that the alarm was even going off. But I've turned it off and I've answered your questions. Can I go now?"

"Sorry, ma'am," the operator said. "Certainly. Have a nice day."

I hung up and turned to my visitors.

"Do you have a permit for that pistol?" Perry asked.

"Yes." I did. I registered my father's illegal piece when I turned eighteen. "I even have a carry permit after I was stalked by this crazy guy from Glendale."

"What happened to him?" the cop asked.

I didn't blame him for asking. He had broken into my home — a policeman. He needed to get some control back. Maybe if he showed some authority I wouldn't bring him up on charges for breaking and entering.

"Fuck that," Lana said in an unusual show of anger. "Where have you been for the last three days?"

"Three days?"

"It's Thursday," Lana said. "Linda's been calling you morning and night. She even made me give her your red phone number."

My red phone.

"I was sleeping," I said. "All those days?"

"You really been asleep all this time?" Lana said.

"What are you doing here, Officer Perry?" I asked.

"Ms. Leer called me."

I looked at the waif-woman.

"It's true," she said. "When you didn't answer I called down to the police department and asked for Mr. Mendelson."

"I'd called twice myself and I was worried," Perry added.

"Worried?"

He looked down at his feet and it felt to me that an empire, somewhere, had crumbled without warning.

"I have to go to the bathroom," I said. "And then I need a bath. Come on."

I led the odd allies through the hallway, past the guest bedroom, leaving them while I went into the smaller bathroom where no one had died.

I went in and did my business, dropped the rest of my clothes on the floor, and then went back to open the door for Lana and Perry. He was surprised to see me naked; I knew he would be. With some men, maybe all men, my sexuality gave me various advantages. Sometimes it was them wanting to take my clothes off; with others they were driven into a shell, seeing my body and not knowing whether to run or to scream.

When I bent over to turn on the bathwater I'm sure Perry looked away.

I took pity on him and poured bubble-bath gel under the stream. Then I climbed in to let the rising water and bubble line slowly hide my dark body.

"Is there any other reason you're here,

Officer?" I asked.

"Um," the policeman uttered.

"What's wrong with you, hon?" Lana asked. "Linda says that if you aren't on the set by this afternoon she's going to fire you."

"Hm," I mused. "How are you, Lana?"

"What?"

"How are you?"

"I understand that your husband's dead and all, baby, but you have commitments."

"Who's that guy?" I said. "The carpenter that works on the sets on all Linda's shoots?"

"Richie," Lana answered, upset to be derailed from her line of questioning.

"Richie — that's right. Call him and ask him to fix the window you guys broke. There's an extra set of keys in the knife drawer in the kitchen. The security code for the alarm system is *bilbo.*"

The bubbles were rising quickly and so Perry chanced a glance in my direction.

"We've identified the woman who was with your husband," he said.

"Oh?"

"Her name was Myrtle May. She was a minor from out near Barstow."

"And how did she know my husband?"

"We haven't figured that out yet."

"Hm."

"Myrtle's mother told us that she found out about her daughter's death from a black woman who came to her home in the late hours of the night a few days ago."

"Really? And what does that have to do with her identity?"

"Was it you?"

"No."

I expected the tightening of his eyes. Seeing this expression made me smile.

"Would you like to put me in a lineup?"

"Why would I want to do that?"

"You seem to think I'm lying."

"What about Linda?" Lana asked me.

"You know, Lana, dear, I haven't shaved my pussy in three days — no, five. It's all stubbly."

"Deb," she pleaded.

"No, honey. I'm not going back. Theon was my husband and I have to bury him and then . . . then I have to settle his affairs."

"You have to work," Lana said, taking on the unwieldy mantle of maturity and logic.

I put my feet up on either side of the tub and laid my head back against the edge. I was still exhausted.

"You haven't met the woman who works harder than I do, babe. You know it; I know it; Linda fuckin' Love does too. I'm tired,

I'm broke, my husband is dead, and I need a moment. Like that guy with the candy bar on the TV commercial."

Perry Mendelson was staring at me now that my nakedness was mostly covered. He was feeling something — what, I couldn't tell.

"Linda's gonna be mad," Lana said again, "real mad."

I wanted to say more but I was too tired under the hot water. I closed my eyes for a minute or so and when I opened them again Lana had gone.

Perry was still there though, still staring.

"Was it you who went out to Barstow in the middle of the night?"

"No."

"I'm not trying to get you in trouble. There's no crime in notifying parents that their daughter has died."

"There is if I was aware of what my husband was doing with an underage minor."

"Did you?"

"No."

"I just want to know what happened."

"Why?" I asked.

"It's my job." The words sounded feeble — no, they sounded distant, as if the man who spoke them had moved past that identity but had not yet picked up a new one.

I realized then that he had somehow identified with me, that the last vestiges of his professionalism had deduced that I had shed an identity the night my husband died.

"Do you want to fuck me, Lieutenant Perry?"

"It's not like that," he said. "That's not why I'm here."

"That's not why you're in a woman's bathroom when she's naked in her tub?"

"You asked me in."

"Do you do everything a woman says?"

Anger replaced innocent confusion in his face.

I laughed. It wasn't a pretty sound.

Perry turned and walked away without another word.

I didn't miss him or Lana. I liked them both but they wanted answers that I either did not have or found intolerable. I was no longer able to function as a proxy for other people's desires.

My life, I felt, was like moisture on the cars and leaves, gates and painted walls of morning. I was evaporating like that dew and I had only a few minutes of life to say good-bye.

I considered putting my head under the water and breathing in. I'd known whores who had killed themselves in that manner.

But I was too drained even to want death. It was too much work to die — hardly worth the effort.

"I want my money," Richard Ness said.

There were one hundred and thirty-nine messages on my phone. He counted for sixteen of them. He never really made a threat, because he knew that could be used against him. He didn't even say my name, just that he wanted his money. In court he could have said that he was calling Theon. He had no proof that my husband was dead. Lieutenant Mendelson hadn't even shown him a badge.

There were dozens of messages from sex workers who had known Theon either through me or from doing business with him. Prince Spear, Mocha Elan, Aphrodite Affair, Darlenee Fox, Johnny "On the Spot" Myles, and many others left their condolences on the tape.

"I heard about Theon from Trixie Ballstrom," Moana Bone said on message seventy-nine. She had been a real porn star back in Theon's day. They had done revolutionary work in the field: quadruple penetrations, multiple simultaneous ejaculations, and possibly the first-ever scene to be done completely underwater.

Moana never failed to forget my name. I don't know if she even recognized me from one chance meeting to the next. Her eyes were always on Theon — willing him to see her as the ravishing beauty of the past.

"I was devastated," Moana continued. "Theon was a wonderful man and I can't imagine what you must be going through. He was so vital when he was young, before you could have known him. What we did together was never pornographic. We weren't just actors; we brought love onto those sets. We brought feeling. . . ."

Her message went on for a full eight minutes. Toward the end she stopped mentioning Theon. There were rock stars and movie stars and political office holders and millionaires whom she spoke of in reference to her career, which, according to her, was far beyond the petty business that I, the current bimbo, was accustomed to.

I listened to every word. I sometimes, even today, replay her monologue. I wasn't angry at her self-centered soliloquy; I wasn't insulted. I didn't laugh at her, because she was the voice of so many men and women who fed the rapacious sexual hunger of the Western world while trying to keep their heads above water.

We have eight young men and a four-hour time slot, a young producer-director once said to me. I'd get seven hundred per come shot — a thousand for every time I swallowed. We all had those kinds of days. How could Moana or anybody else think of their life like that and survive?

"Good afternoon, Mrs. Pinkney," Lewis Dardanelle said at the beginning of message one seventeen. I had been listening to the machine for almost three hours. "Talia has made over seven hundred calls on your husband's behalf and the great majority have offered to donate money or services to the funeral. We have raised, in real dollars, nearly thirty-five thousand. And if the promises are met we will have at least fifty. We, the brothers and I, would like to have the service next Saturday afternoon at two forty-five. If the costs go over the collection, the business will cover the extra expense. Please call or come in anytime after six in the next few days and we will make the arrangements."

There were other messages from Perry Mendelson, Lana and Linda, loan companies and debt reduction services, more porn actors, and one from Marcia Pinkney.

"Hello, dear," the elderly woman said, her

voice frail and ragged. "This is Marcia, your mother-in-law. I heard from one of my church friends that Theon . . . that he passed away. They saw it on the Internet. I'm so sad and so sorry for you. I know we never really got along and I see now that as a Christian I treated you and my son badly. The moment I heard about Theon's transition I realized that I might have helped you and have been closer to my own son if I was not blinded by the feelings I had about your . . . his lifestyle. Now Theon is gone and I can't speak to him. But I hope that you call me and maybe even come see me so that I can make you tea and apologize in person.

"Are you having a funeral? Do you need some help? Please call me, Sandra. God bless you."

Toward the end of the litany of condolences and threats was a message from a man I knew and didn't know. His voice was strained with real emotion.

"Hello, Deb," he said. "This is Jude Lyon. I heard about Theon. Call me if you need to talk or anything else. I'm bereft."

Bereft. That was the word he used. I remember thinking that Jude Lyon was one of the few people I knew who could put that word in a sentence without sounding pompous or awkward.

Jude Lyon was in love with my Theon. He followed him around and did odd jobs for him, and for me too sometimes. Jude was gay but rarely had a lover. Theon was straight but I suspected that he'd had sex with Jude a time or two.

When Theon couldn't make it to pick me up at the airport or accompany me to one of the dozens of porn industry galas, Jude would show up in his vintage BMW dressed in just the right clothes.

Jude loved Theon with an uncritical passion. Though he had no interest in things like baseball, barbecues, or me, he learned to care for these things because Theon did.

"What's up with that guy?" I once asked my husband. "I mean are you two in love or what?"

"It's not like that, babe," he said. We were sitting in the kitchen drinking cognac from juice glasses.

"Then what?"

"You don't want to know too much about JL," he said. "He's probably the most dangerous man I ever met."

"Jude? He doesn't look like he could do five reps with my three-pound dumbbells."

"Don't be fooled; that little faggot could

carry the whole world on his shoulders if he had to."

I asked more, and at other times, but that's all I ever got about Jude and what Theon thought of him.

The last message was from a collection agency. The loan company that Theon was borrowing from was dunning him for a sixteen-thousand-dollar payment. They would repossess everything that he'd put up for collateral: the Humvee, the house, the condo in Aspen, even certain pieces of jewelry that were being held by a third party.

It was like the first page of the first tale in a short-story collection, the first line in a romance of descent.

The red phone was my most precious possession. It was a ruby-colored, semiopaque, glistening cell phone that only a few people had the number of. Built into it was a device that recorded every time someone spoke into the line. It had more than sixty-four gigabytes of memory.

I picked up the little phone in Las Vegas when there was both an adult film convention and a tech convention in the same hotel.

The pasty-faced kid who was in charge of

the spy booth was a young man named Bobby Seaton. I asked him to give me one of the samples and he refused.

"If you give it to me I'll fuck you till the ache in your nuts won't stop for a week."

Bobby wasn't fat but his body was very soft. There was no definition or strength. He insisted on wearing two condoms and had a scared look on his face the whole time we were in his hotel bed.

The only indication he gave that he wanted to be with me was a small, unflagging erection.

"Can, can we stop now?" he asked after his fourth ejaculation.

"Give me the phone," I said.

He hesitated and I grabbed his dick.

He took the phone out of his pants on the floor and handed it to me.

"You can't tell anybody where you got it," he stammered. "It's a federal crime to record phone conversations without consent."

He showed me how to change the chip and use the various features. When he'd finished I reached for his cock again — it was erect immediately.

He actually whimpered.

"Lie down, white boy," I whispered.

He got down on the bed and I fucked him

twice more.

If he'd worn only one condom at a time I don't think I would have tortured him so. I hated his fear but reveled in my power to frighten him. I loved it that he could cringe and orgasm almost simultaneously but I loved that phone even more.

I entered a certain code and was told by the display that I had three unanswered calls from Linda Love's number. I erased them without listening. Then I noticed that the battery was at half power and that the ringer was on. I did a different search and saw that there was another call answered and recorded. . . .

"Hello," Theon said in his faux-distracted tone.

If you knew Theon you knew that this quality of voice was a ploy on his part. He was trying to keep the caller from under-standing his intentions; in this case he didn't want the caller to know that he was secretly spying on me.

My stardom didn't raise envy in Theon's heart but rather he was hungry to share in that success, like an elder in a pride of lions wanted to share in the kill. He must have been overjoyed that I'd forgotten the phone with the ringer on. That way he'd be able to spy on me like a little boy peeking through the keyhole of his mother's boudoir.

"Hi," a girl's voice said — Jolie Wins, Myrtle May. "Is Deb there?"

"She's not in right now," my husband said. "Can I help you?"

"Who, who are you?"

"My name's Axel. I'm Deb's manager. She's out of town and left her phone here at her house. Who's speaking?"

"Jolie. Jolie Wins. Did Deb tell you about me?"

"Jolie? Yeah. Met you the other day at that thing, right? Can I do anything to help?"

"I wanted to ask Deb if maybe there was some kind of job I could do on the set of her new movie. I'm unemployed and they kicked me out of my place. I mean I don't blame 'em. I couldn't pay the rent and so I had to go. Deb's the only kind person I've met in Hollywood. I'd work real hard."

"Well," Theon mused, "like I said, Debbie's out of town on one of her exotic shoots . . . in Tahiti actually."

"Tahiti," Jolie said breathlessly. "Man, I'd love to be there."

"Yeah, me too. But I'll tell you what, Jolie. This is Deb's private line. If you have this number that must mean that you're important to her. So what I'll do is send a car over to get you and bring you here. Maybe I can help you out until Deb gets back. . . ."

They talked a little longer. She was down on Alvarado at a diner. The cook was buying her coffee and doughnuts, probably with the same intentions of my sometimes-slimeball husband. Theon promised to send a limo over to pick her up.

The rest was obvious.

When Theon took one look at Jolie he saw dollar signs and got an erection too. He told her that she could make the same kind of money that I did when I was a kid and that all he had to do was see how she worked on camera. The date on the recording was a week before the two died. He might have been fucking her that whole time for all I knew. Maybe he was putting her up somewhere, promising her a starring role in his upcoming feature-length adult masterpiece.

It was my fault. I should have kept tabs on her. Or I should have ignored her at the hip-hop party and let her find her own way down. Instead I gave her false hope and a phone number that Theon had access to.

I had killed them both.

"Hello," Kip Rhinehart said, answering his phone.

"Hey, Kip, it's me — Deb."

"Hey, babe. Long time no see."

"I been kinda busy."

"I know, big important woman like you. What can I do for you?"

"I was just wondering . . ."

"Yeah?"

"Did Theon have a girl in one of your rooms up there?"

"I heard he died," Kip said.

"Yeah. Him and this sixteen-year-old. They let a camera fall in the bathtub and electrocuted themselves while fucking."

"That's hard."

"Was she there?"

Silence.

"Come on now, Kip," I said. "He's dead. She's dead. There's no one left to protect. You're the first person Theon'd call if he needed to put up someone on the QT."

"Yeah. She had one of the garden rooms. Nice kid. Fucked-up, but she was nice. Had manners, you know?"

"I'm gonna wanna see the room and her stuff," I said.

"Sure, Deb. Nothing worth anything there but I'll lock it up until you come."

"I'll drop by tonight or at the latest tomorrow morning."

"Whenever. I'm here day and night."

After calling Kip I lost steam for a while again. My life was in its uphill phase (a term I once read in a self-help book). Every step I took was a strain. I wanted to go to bed but I knew that I'd sleep for another three days if I did.

So I sat in the polar bear room staring at the thick white carpeting.

"How do you feel, Deb?" I asked after twenty or more minutes had passed.

"Like shit."

An hour went by. I began registering sounds from various sources. There was ticking from an antique porcelain couple fornicating on the white marble end table. Theon had bought the little sculpture for me but I never realized that the platinum disk on the side was also a clock.

One of the fourteen environmentally friendly ceiling lights was whining softly. A strong breeze was blowing and the sliding glass doors that led to the patio and swimming pool rumbled gently on their tracks.

I realized that I'd agreed on buying the house because it resembled the home of the shoot I'd done in the south of France — the one I dreamed about.

Why hadn't I known that?

"Really, Deb," I said. "How are you?

"I'm cut off," I said. "A junkie in paradise. A bitch in heat locked in a room full of doggie dolls.

"Write that down."

I don't usually talk to myself. As a matter of fact I had never done so (or at least I don't remember doing it) before that day. But I got up and went to the kitchen where our housekeeper, Mrs. Slatkin, usually kept a blank book diary where she wrote down the things she wanted us to buy. This little journal was fairly new. Only a few pages had been scribbled on. I tore out the used sheets and jotted down the words I'd asked myself to write.

Only the first few words, *I'm cut off,* seemed to go anywhere. A junkie in paradise was more like a book or movie title, and a bitch in heat locked in a room full of doggie dolls used too many words to get the point across.

My father's midnight special was on the kitchen table next to where I wrote. I was wondering about the significance of this, this juxtaposition, when the doorbell sounded.

It was the first nineteen notes from Beethoven's Seventh Symphony. That was the only classical music that Theon knew. He'd loved it as the orchestration of the Sean Connery movie *Zardoz*.

I put the pistol in the pocket of my tatty blue-and-yellow dress and wandered up toward the front door thinking that everything was connected but, at the same time, nothing mattered.

She was tall and austere-looking in her navy blue, calf-length dress suit and maroon high-heeled shoes. Dr. Anna Karin was ten years older than I but in some ways her face seemed younger, at least more innocent. She smiled when I opened the door. I could imagine why. When last she saw me I was in a tight red vinyl minidress with white hair nearly down to my tailbone. My eyes were oceanic blue and I had glossy platinum-colored nails longer than a toddler's fingers.

"Hello, Sandra," she said.

Karin was born in Copenhagen but she didn't have an accent. Her enunciation was very, very American, more so than most people you meet who were born here. That was how I could tell that she wasn't — American, that is.

We met when I was going through a bout of anorexia. Theon was afraid that I'd hurt my health (and our income) and so he got

Karin's name from one of his legit Hollywood friends.

"A house call?" I said.

"I was concerned."

We stood at the threshold staring at each other — the handsome Scandinavian and I.

I wondered why she was there and what my black skin would look like next to hers. This latter thought wasn't sexual musing but professional reflex. How women looked on a set when paired up with one or many men often made a scene work.

But I was retired.

"Come on in," I said, turning my back and leading her into the white-on-white-in-white living room.

"Have a seat," I offered, and she lowered herself into one of the three oversize stuffed chairs that were upholstered in lambskin.

"This room is quite stark," she said. "Is it your husband's design?"

"No. This is the only room in the house that I'm responsible for."

"You look very different."

"So do you."

"How do you mean?" Anna asked, holding her hands up a few inches, indicating the space around her as if it were a permanent aura.

"I've never seen you outside of your office before."

"How are you, Sandra?"

"I haven't shaved my pussy for days. It itches."

"What does that mean to you?"

"No," I said.

"No?"

"You're a visitor in my house, Anna. I'm not on your couch; I haven't asked for a session. If you want to be a friend I'm happy to offer you some wine or mineral water. I'll even make an omelet if you're hungry. But I will not be psychoanalyzed in my own home — by a guest."

Ideas and convictions were already coming out of me and I'd only written a few words in my journal.

"What happened?" Anna asked.

I told her the story of Theon and Jolie, of Big Dick and my first orgasm in years, of the gangster, the cop, and Rash Vineland, who could get me to talk like no one had in a very long time.

"I don't want to sound like a therapist in your own home," Anna said. "But you sound so detached. It's like you have no connection to these tragedies or any other feelings."

"I'm a spiritual paraplegic," I agreed. "I'm

stuck, cut off, and numb."

Concern creased the sophisticated brow of the descendant of bloodthirsty Vikings.

"What can I do?" she asked.

"I'm broke, Anna. That's why I didn't return your call. Theon spent all our money, every cent, before he died. I can't afford to see you. In a couple of months I won't even have my own bed to sleep in."

For a long while she stared at me. I thought that she was looking for a friendly way to excuse herself. The world we lived in was defined by the ability to pay, and I no longer had that talent. Her accent alone was enough to tell me that she couldn't, that she wouldn't and even shouldn't reach out across the void of poverty.

"I work from eight in the morning until five every afternoon," Anna said after a long span of silence. "You can choose any two mornings at six and I will be there to meet with you."

"I don't need two mornings," I said, a little breathless with gratitude, not in appreciation for the free offer of therapy but for the generosity itself. I might have been near tears.

"Yes, you do," Anna Karin said. "As a matter of fact I will only agree to see you if you consent to meeting me twice a week."

"I don't understand."

Anna's eyes were a pale blue, like a day that had been bright but was now being covered by a thin layering of clouds.

She smiled.

"I don't want you to leave yet," I said then, realizing that she wasn't going to answer my question.

She sat back in the plush chair and eyed me closely.

I enjoyed the scrutiny. This made me think of the pleasure Lana got when I gazed so closely at her.

"I know you don't," Anna said. "But there's a delicate line here. We are about to embark upon a very fragile phase of our relationship. This is not about friendship. A friend would not be able to break the bond that you're held by. A friend would not be able to let you go."

Again I felt something. There was some kind of truth in her statement. I knew what she said was right but I couldn't have explained why.

Anna stood up then and nodded.

"Wednesday and Thursday," I said, because it was a week away and I needed time.

"Six in the morning," Anna added.

"Do you have to go?"

"Yes," she said. "I do."

The next thing I knew I was on my feet holding Anna with all my might. She gripped me in an embrace that was almost a restraint. I was surprised by her strength.

We let go at the same moment, as if the movements had been choreographed.

"I will see you this coming Wednesday," she said. "Six a.m."

I watched as she walked away, unable to bring myself to accompany her to the door.

I got to Threadley's at a little after nine that evening. The door was locked, so I pressed the bell and waited patiently. Lewis Dardanelle was somewhere inside. He was like a vampire who only came out to work at night. Most of the people he met were by appointment only.

I was still wearing the faded dress and tattered sneakers. But I had showered and so felt presentable.

"Mrs. Pinkney," a voice spoke from a speaker embedded in the wall.

"Yes, Mr. Dardanelle. I'm here about your call."

"I'll be right down." His voice was crisp, almost buoyant.

I thought about my mother. She still lived in the small house where I was raised, off Central Avenue, down around Watts. I wouldn't be able to send her any more checks. That would make my older brother, Cornell, happy. He always wanted to be seen as the breadwinner of our family but I was the one who supported Mom. I wondered how Cornell was, if he'd speak to me ever again.

The extra-wide door of the mortuary swung inward and the lean mortician bowed for me to enter.

"Let's go to my office," he said with a wan and yet somehow a profound smile. Or maybe I was just reading things into every gesture and motion; maybe the only truth in my world was a fabrication perpetrated by a state of shock.

He led me through the barren stone room to a small hallway. At the end of this shabby lane of coffin-lid-thin doors we came to a small elevator. It was crowded in there with just the two of us.

The vestibule moved slowly past the second floor and the third. I could hear Dardanelle's bellowslike breath coming slowly and strong.

"He wants to what?" I had asked Theon one evening when he had come home from planning the burial of Sack "Big Daddy" Pounds.

"He wants to have sex with you in this special coffin he keeps in a room next to his office," Theon said, as if my answer were a foregone conclusion. "He says that he'll give us Sack's coffin at half off if we do."

"We?"

Passing the fourth floor of the six-story house of death I was brought back to the night Theon expected me to whore for his dead friend. I considered walking out, calling Theon a bastard, breaking the glass I held in my hand. It wasn't so much that I was appalled by Lewis or by having sex with someone and being paid for it. Almost every woman I knew considered the monetary value of the man she took off her clothes for.

What upset me was the thought of having to fuck for money after I died (even if that death was only a metaphor), of being lowered into a coffin and having some man with a hard-on put on top of me instead of a cool muslin shroud.

I wanted to scream and run from the image Theon had conjured up for our death-house discount, but instead a pastel calm came over me.

"Theon," I said, looking into his eyes with my head cocked and my fake blue eyes beaming.

He saw in me the turmoil of a life under hot lights, of marriage to a man who was sometimes no better than a pimp, of sores and viruses and intimacies that no living being could endure without some kind of protection.

I saw my thoughts roll around behind his eyes and he saw me observing his most vulnerable insights.

"I'm sorry, babe," he said.

When we went to bed that night he held me and kissed my neck.

There was a cricket somewhere in the house calling out for a mate. I smiled at the memory of a husband who, for all his flaws, managed to get it right every once in a while.

"Here we are," Lewis Dardanelle said.

The elevator had stopped and the towering man was holding the door for me.

I wondered why I wasn't afraid. Why hadn't I, in years, felt the tremors of fear around violent men who hated women with their sex and their words?

Slap her tits while you're fucking that cunt, one director said in every scene I did for him, and I did four scenes a day, three days a week for eighteen months.

Dardanelle's office contained the dark and cool calm of a peaceful dream about to end. His desk was white ash and there were paintings of flowers hung on every wall. There was no bookcase, just a round oak table with various religious texts strewn upon it.

"Let's sit at the table," Lewis said, gesturing for me to choose a seat.

He sat after I did, lacing his arachnidlike fingers and smiling just under the threshold of humor.

"We have received sixty-eight thousand dollars in cash and credit card accounts," he said, explaining the smile's nature with these words.

"That's wonderful."

"We could take the big chapel up at Day's Rest."

"I like the idea of having the service near the grave," I said. "How many people have given money?"

"Four hundred and ninety-eight."

"Then we should plan on a service for, say . . . seven hundred?"

"Yes."

"I guess the big room would be appropriate then."

"Yes. Would you like to view coffins this evening?"

"No."

"No?"

"I want him in a plain pine box, Lew. Light wood with no flourishes, no finish, if you can find something like that."

"I'm sure we have something."

"Take what's left from the service and get Talia to see to the catering at our house. You have the address?"

"Yes."

"I'll get Lana Leer to call Talia. I'll give Lana the key, so all they have to do is work out the logistics."

Dardanelle and I were as peaceful as the grave; there was no conflict among the dead.

We sat there in the soft light of the silent office. Now and then an errant sound wafted up from the street.

I don't remember leaving Threadley's that evening: not standing up from the round table or saying good night, not thanking Lewis for the work he and Talia had done or filling out the papers that I must have signed. The next thing I knew I was pulling into my driveway, wondering if Richard Ness would be waiting for me.

The night passed like waves that back up on themselves and then press forward again. This feeling was in the form of dreams and half-conscious musings. The ideas from both states of awareness traded places, moved back and forth almost as if I were a fabricated notion of some other being who had conjured me as a character in fiction or a play.

The character, me — young Sandy Peel — was fifteen and on the run from the police. I had been giving blow jobs in a parking lot south of Hollywood Boulevard and the cops were cracking down on that activity. My best friend at the time, Amy Chapman, had been arrested and sent to jail for thirty days even though she was my age.

I saw the cops and they saw me. I went through a wire gate into an alley that split into three directions. I went straight ahead, climbed into a backyard where a dog tried to bite me, and made it to the boulevard. I walked into a chain coffee shop and took a seat at a table where a man was drinking expensive coffee served in a paper cup.

"Excuse me," I said to the gentleman. "Can I sit here with you for a little while?"

"You solo?" he asked.

"Huh?"

He smiled at my naïveté.

His smile made me mad and I would have gotten up and left, but I saw the uniforms that had been chasing me right outside the coffee shop window.

The man saw my fear and its source with a glance and moved his chair so that his body blocked me from being seen.

"My name is Theon Pinkney," he said.

He was around forty, ancient to my teen-age eyes, wearing gray slacks and a maroon dress shirt open to show off his chest hair.

"I'm Debbie Dare," I said, making up a whole new life then and there.

"My car's in the parking lot out back," he said. "Would you like me to drive you somewhere?"

"Out from this life into another one where a girl could hit a break," I said.

I had heard these words from Mela David, an older prostitute who sometimes threw work our way. If all a guy wanted was a fifteen-dollar blow job, she'd send him to the parking lot that Amy and I haunted.

Theon smiled and gestured toward the back of the restaurant with his right hand. He wore three thick gold rings, with a single gem embedded in each: one ruby, one emerald, and a yellow diamond. The brightness of those jewels took my breath away.

He drove a red Rolls with the softest calf-skin seats I ever sat in.

He reached over and pulled my seat belt

on for me. This was also a first in my experience. Every other time I got in a strange man's car it was to suck his dick, and you couldn't do that in a harness.

As he turned left onto Hollywood he asked, "Now, where is this life you were talking about?"

"Where you live at?" I asked, and he smiled again.

"Do you know who I am?"

"No."

"You ever watch X-rated movies?"

"Sometimes I be wit' a boyfriend who watch 'em but I never paid much mind."

"I bet it takes a lot to impress you."

"I like your rings," I said with some emphasis.

"How old are you?"

"Old enough to get arrested for suckin' a white man's dick in the front seat'a his car."

"Do they arrest the man?"

"No. They give him a summons an' send him home."

"They should arrest the john for child molesting and send you home to your mother."

"I ain't no child."

"Only a child could be as beautiful as you are, Debbie Dare."

I was very young and he was older than

my dead father but that didn't matter. The place I was looking for was a room where somebody looked at me and called me pretty. I was a wild thing when I climbed into Theon Pinkney's car but he tamed me with just a few words.

When I woke up the morning sun was streaming into the polar bear room. There was drool down the side of my face and my crotch itched.

In the bathroom I peered into the mirror, half expecting to see white roots coming in at the baseline of my brown hair.

I brushed my teeth and ran a comb through the short dark brown mane.

There were three messages on the answering machine. I wondered if I had missed them when I got home, or maybe the phone had rung in the night but I was too deep asleep to hear it.

Marcia Pinkney had called again. She said that she'd be home for the entire day tomorrow and would be happy to see me at any time.

I wondered again at the time of her call. It was ten in the morning and Marcia was an early riser. If the call had come in on Thursday then she meant for me to drop by today; if it was this morning that she called she'd be expecting a Saturday visit.

This displaced feeling fit perfectly with my state of mind. I was lost in time, experiencing the past as clearly as (in some cases more so than) the present.

For long minutes I considered Marcia Pinkney's call and its origins. It didn't occur to me to call her. Marcia had never spoken to me directly. When Theon brought me to her home, on the occasion of his brother's death, she had said to Theon, "Please tell this woman that she is not welcome in my home."

Finally I moved on to the second message.

"You're fired!" Linda Love shouted, and then she slammed her receiver down.

"Coco Manetti here," the third caller said, his voice smooth and somewhat sinister. "I'm an associate of Richard Ness. . . ." He left a number and said that he hoped I would call him.

I knew of Coco. I'd have to shoot him if ever I brought out my father's piece.

A pang of hunger made its presence known. I was starving. This feeling confused me. For so long I went hungry by choice.

LeRoy's Chicken and Waffle House was on Venice Boulevard very near the ocean. Absolutely everybody ate there at one time or other.

I had the pecan waffle with two spicy thighs and a side of hash browns along with coffee and orange juice.

I sat at an outside table that faced in a westerly direction but did not afford the view of the ocean; it was just that much too far away.

The sky was clear and vacant like nearly every day in Los Angeles, like most of the people who came to California.

The feeling of Los Angeles is that of free fall, I wrote in the little journal that I pilfered from our housekeeper. *There's nothing to grab onto but it's beautiful if you could only stop and appreciate the view.*

It felt good eating all that food and sitting outside in the stupid but beautiful day. No one came to talk to me because of my dress and shoes. It was the perfect disguise in that part of L.A., the shabby, faded look.

Hey, Debbie, I remembered a male fan once shouting at an adult film event, *I just wanna fuck that red dress, baby, that's all.*

Kip Rhinehart lived in a converted schoolhouse way up a steep driveway deep in Malibu Canyon. It was a horseshoe-shaped building with the hump facing toward the entrance drive. The arc of the front of the building was two stories high. Kip had an apartment on the second floor. The rest of the place was composed of single-story classrooms. These were leased by the day or week to people in various businesses, including my own.

I parked behind Kip's red pickup in the circular area in front of the informal business. Then I rang the doorbell and waited patiently.

You could smell the ocean up there — something to do with the wind currents. There was a wildness to that particular section of the canyon that almost made it seem alive — not filled with life but like a huge creature with a single mind and a long, long life span.

"Can I help you?" a man called from my right.

He would have been shorter than I even standing straight, but Kip was a little hunched over from some natural malady or condition. He wore a white T-shirt and dark blue jeans. He also had on hard-looking light brown cowboy boots.

"Hey, Kip."

"Yes?"

"Don't you recognize me?"

The sixty-year-old's face was wrinkled and brownish but he was a white guy. When he

131

squinted he aged a decade. The surprise made him younger again.

"Deb? That you?"

"Do I have to put on a wig and contact lenses just to come visit?"

"No," he said.

He rushed over and hugged me.

Kip was one of the few men I allowed this privilege. Guys tried to grab me so often that I naturally avoided cuddles, clinches, and bear hugs. But with Kip it was always friendly, considerate.

"What happened to your hair?" he asked.

"I'm just tired, Kip."

The empathy in his eyes reflected some decision that he'd reached long ago, before I was born no doubt.

"You wanna cup'a java?" he asked.

Kip's property ended at a cliff that overlooked the ocean. The tiny bands of waves were far enough away that you could see but not hear them.

There was a stone dais laid out at the far edge. On this platform sat a pink table and four shabby plastic white chairs. It was there that Kip served me his Spanish coffee and canned evaporated milk.

I accepted this hospitality not because I wanted or needed it but because he offered.

The kindness was like a high-denomination poker chip: valueless as a thing but representing something of significance.

"I'm so sorry about Theon," he said after we were seated and looking out.

It was early afternoon. The sun was high and hot.

"He went out with a beautiful girl on top of him," I replied.

"He loved you though."

"Yeah. I guess he did."

"It's hard being an old porn star, Deb," Kip said. "I mean, it's harder on women but guys feel it too. There's no retirement plan and unless they can use a camera there's no work to speak of."

"It's quiet around here," I said, because there was no reply to Kip's pronouncement.

"Not rentin' out too much. I took in Jolie 'cause Theon asked personally. Place is paid for and I got my government check for the bills."

Kip gazed back at the vacant area inside the horseshoe. It was a brick playground turned patio, with grasses and weeds growing up through the cracks. Looking at that space I remembered seeing Kip gazing down from his second-floor window when I was taking one man's hard-on down my

133

throat while his German friend was fucking my ass.

"I was chokin' at one end and trying to relax at the other," I told Theon that night.

He told me that he'd been in the exact same situation once when a gambler, Coco Manetti, made him do a gay film to pay off a bad debt.

I remembered feeling sorry for Theon.

And now he was dead.

"It's good that you quittin' the business," Kip said. "That's no kind of life for you."

"No kind of life for anyone."

"But you're so smart, Deb," he argued. "A lotta these people in the life couldn't be anything else. At least they get paid for bein' young and flexible. But you read books . . . you talk like you know somethin'.

"I remember when I first met you, when you were just a kid. You talked like you were straight outta the hood, but now you talk like some kinda coed or somethin'."

Theon had paid for my etiquette lessons.

"How do you know I read?" I asked. I never talked about books to anyone except my therapist and that one arrogant literature professor.

"Theon told me. I asked him did he get jealous with you havin' sex with all those young men and he said that it was only the

134

books made him turn green. He said that he always felt like he was about to lose you when you were lookin' in a book."

The window of Jolie's room looked down the cliff and over the Pacific. It was the kind of place that only wealth or beauty could afford. My family and I had lived in a small cottage. There was no privacy, much less solace, and the only view was of the street and smoggy city sky. What little green we had was painted on the concrete of our front yard. But I was never bothered by any of that. I adored my brothers, took care of my mother, and my father was a dream come true. He read me fairy tales and showed me how to count money when he was still comfortable with me sitting on his lap.

I was remembering the scent of Aldo Peel as I sat on Jolie's last bed. Aftershave and deodorant, tobacco smoke and whiskey — the feeling of my father could still steal up on me and transform, for an instant, wherever I was into the home I abandoned.

There was a small stack of magazines under the bed. Style and fashion publications that showed off beautiful women with handsome men, along with the chic clothes and gorgeous architecture.

Myrtle May had read these glossy maga-zines closely and voraciously; I could tell this by the wrinkled pages and sentences that had been underlined in pink ink throughout.

Beauty, one such underlined passage read, *is a thing that rises out from the inside of a person. A man will be attracted by form and style but this inner beauty is what he lives for.*

Your body is the bank, another sentence said, *but the wealth is your spirit.*

There were many such lines in the beauty magazines. This surprised me. I read the same publications and couldn't remember having come across such insightful com-ments.

She had cigarettes and a joint in her desk drawer, quaaludes and a tiny bag of cocaine in a small lacquered box on the bureau. Her childish jewelry was either silver or gold plated. Her clothes were jumbled in a box on the floor.

There was a violet diary with a stylized red heart and yellow flower stenciled across the cover. There was a small latch that she had locked. The key was probably with the police, or maybe her parents had it now.

I had just pulled out of Kip's driveway when I decided to drive off the road and crash my car down the cliff and into the Pacific. It wasn't a difficult choice; nor was it a judgment or verdict. It was like deciding to listen to jazz after five years of rock and roll, like changing the radio station after renting a car in a different city.

I was just going to drive off the road. There was no trepidation or physical awareness; I wasn't afraid of the pain.

Up ahead of me, just beyond the turn there was a clear view of the sky. That's where I was going to fly off. When I got there and made the turn, I found myself on a little area designed for motorists to pull off when they got lost. The cliff was guarded by trees and three big boulders.

There was no egress (a word I once read in a nineteenth-century romance). I had to stop.

And when I stopped the entirety of the days since that orgasm, since those senseless deaths, since I'd lost everything I'd worked for for fifteen years and more — it all crashed in from behind, like a bulldozer trying to push me over the edge.

I had never cried like that before. Even the heartrending loss of my father didn't call up such grief. I screamed so hard that I couldn't breathe, cried so violently that it felt like my insides would come out of my eyes, nose, and mouth.

I flung the car door open and threw myself from the seat. Falling to the ground I willed myself to stand, then lurched stiff-legged to the gap between the boulders and looked down.

I remembered every sensation, sound, and smell as if I were experiencing them at this very moment. There was the chattering birdsong from the bushes below, but Death filled the horizon. I remembered smashing my favorite doll after my mother came home from the emergency room and told me that my father was dead. It was a fancy, old-fashioned black doll that he had given me.

"Niggahs done kill him," Mom's friend Galia said.

I destroyed that doll, hoping the sacrifice would somehow reverse time and bring my father back. I was a mad scientist and an angry child. But now, overlooking the ocean, all I could do was cry.

I sat down between the guard stones and wept. The misery in me was hot wax over an unrelenting flame. I was being consumed by my own fires. My soul, I felt, was dripping down that mountainside between the bushes and birds, ants and hidden animals. I was a husk then, an empty vessel that had been filled with poisons.

When it was over I was both drained and clear. I felt like the inner-city sky after the rains had washed away the pollution. I stood up, experiencing a sensation of weightlessness. The sorrow was gone from me but I had no reason to smile. The spiritual infection that drained out of me on that little turnabout had been inside for years. Cutting off my hair had been like pressing the wound but not treating it. Days of sleep only served to deaden but not destroy the pain.

I'd left Kip's residence at two-oh-two that afternoon. It was two twenty-eight when I got back in the car.

While driving down the canyon road I thought of my mother hanging clothes to dry on the line in the backyard. She'd usually have a radio playing old disco songs while she danced with the sheets and T-shirts, bras and socks.

"Why you always got to be washin' clothes an' hangin' 'em up on a line, Mama?" my younger brother, Newland, asked for at least the hundredth time.

My mother never got tired of the question. She'd always answer, "You have to wash 'em sometimes, baby; otherwise they get all stinky and stiff."

Marcia Pinkney's home sat between two other flat-roofed houses in the dead-end arc of a cul-de-sac on a street named Pine Circle. The grass was green and trimmed and the front porch was the length of the front of the ultramodern-looking house. I parked in the driveway and walked across the lawn.

The blue tennis shoes were worn and so I could feel moisture from a recent watering through the soles and sides of the shoes. The cold spots made me smile. I stopped to appreciate this sensation.

The sky above my head was gray from air pollution. A gang of starlings squabbled madly in the limbs of a great oak standing in the left-side neighbor's yard.

Somewhere, I was sure, a black woman in a white wig was rutting under the high school dreams of Myron Palmer or one of his friends. The woman in the wig would certainly steal my name.

I willed myself to take a step but my legs resisted. I took a deep breath and leaned forward — if my legs refused I'd fall to the ground. Half the way into the fall my right leg jutted forward and I was again stalking toward Theon's mother's home.

The door was open but the screen was shut.

I pressed the button and chimes filled the air.

Inside the house was dark, shadowy. It was hot outside but cool air was rushing out through the screen.

It came to me that I should walk away at that moment. This was the only appropriate action to take.

"Hello, dear," Marcia Pinkney said.

She was standing in the haze of the screen door, neither smiling nor frowning, staring into my face.

"You look different," the slender and small white woman said.

"Can I come in?" I hadn't spoken since leaving Kip's house.

"Of course," the older woman said as she undid a latch and pulled the door open. "Do you have a cold, dear?"

"I've been crying," I said.

"Oh . . . yes, of course."

Theon's mother was short and frail-looking. The white of her dress made her skin seem gray. Her bones were made for birds and other slight creatures but her eyes were dark and magnificent.

She led me through the unlit rooms that

were not walled off from one another. To the left was a sunken living room that had green carpeting and violet walls. To the right the kitchen lay. It was a brown-on-brown affair with tall stools and a plank apron that went around three sides of the stove.

Marcia led me through the house to a double yellow door that opened onto a covered patio, which looked out on a waterless swimming pool. The bottom of the pool was littered with dry brown leaves and caked with dirt.

"Something to drink?" Theon's mother asked me.

A crystal pitcher sat on the coral-colored aluminum table. Sweating, it was filled with a bright green liquid.

"Gin and sweet lime," she said, as if introducing me to a sentient being.

The baby-blue chairs were made from some kind of space-age ceramic material. It felt like I had to press myself down just to sit. I still had the feeling of weightlessness. As if in a dream I imagined that I could float up above the roof and sail away to Hawaii or even farther — to lands that had not yet been discovered.

There was a silver tray with two unbreakable clear plastic tumblers on it. Marcia poured the tumblers full and handed one to me.

I took a sip. It was very sweet and tangy, not alcoholic at all.

"Were you expecting someone?" I asked.

"You, my dear."

"Oh?" I felt complimented and at the same time compromised.

"Where do I begin?" Marcia asked.

"The funeral is set for next Saturday at Day's Rest."

"Oh." I could see her thinking of the zoo the memorial service would be.

"You could come the night before to say good-bye if you wanted," I offered.

"Theon told me that you were very perceptive," she said through a mild smile. "But I didn't listen to him. I never listened to him."

She took a deep gulp from the glass.

I did the same.

"Did you love him?" she asked.

"Often but not always."

"I blamed you for destroying his life."

"When Theon and I met he was forty-three and I had just turned fifteen."

The math pained her. She took a drink and I responded in kind.

"That young?"

"He always liked younger women."

"You were a child."

"Not on the street I wasn't. I couldn't afford to be."

"I . . ." she said, and then took another drink.

I swigged my gin Kool-Aid and waited for the rest.

"I can't . . . I can't bear to think about these things in my house," Marcia Pinkney said at last. "I told Theon that I didn't want his sordid business here."

"He was born here, Marcia."

"I know."

We both finished our sweet drinks and she refilled our glasses.

I felt the mental stutter of inebriation when I looked up to see a jet flying high above.

"What was he like?" Marcia asked.

I gazed at her, nearly flummoxed by the question.

"Did he collect stamps?" she added. "Did he play softball?"

"Didn't you ever talk to him?"

"When his father was alive . . ." she said, and then paused. "When his father was alive there was a lot of conflict between them."

Henry Pinkney beat his sons mercilessly. That was why Theon never wanted children. *My dad would beat us and Mom would leave the house,* he'd told me more than once. *My idea of family is going to the park and watching other people play with their kids.*

"When Hank died," Marcia continued, "I thought that things would get better, but Johnny ran away and Theon turned angry and sullen. I tried to talk to him but he wouldn't listen. He got that apartment in Hollywood and met that . . . that awful woman, that Moana Bone. She was the one who turned him into a pimp."

Marcia didn't know the right words but I understood what she meant. And anyway, in the end Theon had actually become a pimp of sorts.

"It must have been terrible to feel like you were losin' your fam'ly one at a time," I said. The liquor had affected my words. My mother's tongue was speaking for me.

I felt like a field of wheat undulating under the pressure of otherwise imperceptible breezes.

"Oh yes," Marcia said with certainty. "I wished that I had a daughter to sit with me."

"Girl might not be what you wanted neither, Marcia. Moana Bone was somebody's little girl once."

"Her mother must curse the day she was born," my mother-in-law said.

"Just like you and Theon."

The widow gave me a grieved look and refilled both our glasses.

"Am I really so evil?" she asked.

"I wish none of it ever happened," I replied.

"Don't we all," she agreed.

"No, Mrs. Pinkney," I said. "No. A lot of people love their hate. They live to hate the people wronged them. You cain't just have one gang. That don't even make sense. If you took away the white man's black man or the black man's white man, most of 'em wouldn't even know how to walk down the street right."

Marcia Pinkney started and stared. She shivered and almost forgot to take a swig of her sweet oblivion.

"I hated you because you were a black girl," she said, as if it were a revelation — even to her.

"I know that."

"You do?"

"Yeah."

"How could you know when I only just realized it right now?"

"Theon told me that when he hooked up wit' Moana you went to her and begged that she let Theon go. He said you offered her money and anything else she wanted. But when he finally did leave her and got to-

146

gether with me you didn't even try."

I could see that Marcia wanted to deny my slurred indictment, that she wanted to say that it was a different time and situation. But she couldn't put the lie into words.

"I'm so sorry," she said, and then she began to weep.

I got a little teary too. Not the racking anguish I felt on the mountainside. This was more like a gentle mist than a raging storm. But still it moved me enough to get up and go over to Marcia. I knelt down next to her ceramic chair and embraced her. She was stiff at first but then let go and cried on my shoulder.

After a few minutes of these soft tears she patted my arm and I went back to my chair. We divvied up the last of the delicious drink and stared out over the empty, filthy pool into the polluted sky, through which we could see the bare outline of the San Bernardino Mountains.

The sun was going down but it was comfortable enough outside.

A trio of hummingbirds came by to inspect the scent of the now empty pitcher. Marcia snored gently as I watched the delicate birds inspect this wonderful but inaccessible plastic flower.

One of them did a circuit around my

head. Maybe she smelled the sugar on my lips. I thought that it would be nice to be kissed by a hummingbird.

Soon they all flitted away to a bush of yellow flowers on the far side of the pool.

Not long after that the sun began to set. I was sad and peaceful sitting there.

"Oh dear," Marcia said after a while.

"What, Mrs. Pinkney?"

"I can't seem to stand up."

"Is something wrong?"

"I think it's the gin," she said, and then chuckled.

I giggled along with her.

"Let me help you," I said.

I tried to get up but failed on the first attempt. Taking a deep breath I tried once more, stood up, and stayed in that posture. I found that I could maintain that stance as long as I held on to the edge of the aluminum table.

"Your sheets are in the wind too," Marcia said.

I wondered if the words actually meant what she was saying. It didn't matter — the old racist and I understood each other quite well.

"I should put you to bed," I said.

I helped Marcia Pinkney to her feet and walked with her to the many-windowed master bedroom. I helped her off with the white dress and laid her down, pulling the blankets up to her chin.

I thought she had fallen back asleep but then she grabbed my hand.

"Don't go when you're still tipsy, dear," she said.

"Don't you worry," I said. "I'll sit out on the couch and watch TV until I'm sober enough to drive."

In the living room I contemplated watching the old console television but gave up the notion. Just the idea of the jangled sounds and shifting images made me queasy. I sat on an ugly maroon couch that was built to seat two. On a green stone table next to it was a framed photograph of Theon when he was maybe thirteen. He was smiling with his mouth but not his eyes. I saw in the child the future man.

This vision brought a sigh from deep in my lungs.

I cradled the picture and sat back on the unsightly but comfortable couch.

It was so strange to be out in Pomona sharing confidences with Theon's mother. One of the reasons he married me was that he knew that she and I could never be friends. Theon didn't trust his mother. He believed that she could have saved him from his father's savage beatings but that she did not because she didn't love him enough. This distinction was very important to him: His mother did love him but not enough to save him.

Smiling at the thought of my dead husband's delicate psyche I closed my eyes. When I opened them again the sky had lightened. The sun was not yet up but dawn was coming.

I stumbled out to my car and popped the trunk. There I kept a small leather bag with all my toiletries. I brought this into the house, found a guest toilet far from Marcia's bedroom, and did my morning cleanup.

At least I didn't have to shave.

Before leaving I peeked in on Marcia. With her defenses of nostalgia and gin she was able to appear somewhat in charge of her diminishing domain. But sleep took away her armor, leaving an old woman bereft of everything she'd lived for.

I thought about the word *bereft* and remembered Jude Lyon. When Theon had told me that Jude was dangerous there was actual fear in his tone.

I left a note on the kitchen table with my red phone number on it. Then I walked out into the weak sunshine of early morning, put the toiletry bag back into the trunk, and made it to the driver's seat. There I closed the car door but had to stay still for a few moments in deference to my body's memory of the alcohol.

My head ached and there was a buzzing in my ear.

I considered letting the seat back and napping for a while before driving off.

A few more minutes passed.

Then there came a tapping on the window.

I turned and saw a uniformed policeman. He'd rapped on my glass with his nightstick. In the side-view mirror I could see at least two other cops approaching.

I was that fifteen-year-old girl again, praying for a Theon Pinkney to help me escape.

The cop motioned for me to roll down the window.

An instantaneous chemical reaction purged me of the hangover.

I opened the car door.

"I said to put down the window." The cop raised his voice enough for the tones to shift while he was speaking.

"To do that I'd have to turn the ignition," I said, back in full control of my tongue.

"Get out," he commanded.

I smiled, swiveled, and stood.

"Lift your hands at your side," another policeman said.

I'd had a hundred directors telling me what to do with my body parts. These were just two more.

The first cop was white — they all were white — and male. He, the first one, went into the car while the second director turned me around, pushed my arms down behind my back, and put handcuffs on my wrists. I let my body go limp in order to minimize the bruising from the adrenaline-filled police.

I was turned around, not gently.

"You broke into this home," a gray-headed policeman told me. He wore reflective sunglasses and had almost indiscernible gray stubble on his chin. His breath was both minty and sour.

"No. I was visiting my mother-in-law," I said. "Now I'm going home."

"Yeah, sure," the cop said. "We got the call from a neighbor that a black woman was breaking into her neighbor's home, taking things from the house and putting them in her trunk."

My big blue bag was in the trunk with my father's gun inside. I had a carry permit in my wallet, but if the constabulary was not inclined to believe me then they didn't have

152

to believe my documents either.

If my hair was long and white and my eyes the color of the ocean they would have recognized me immediately, maybe asked for an autograph. I wrote these words in my little journal not long after that encounter. Of course, now I realize that if I were a white woman driving a pale blue Jaguar the cops would have never put cuffs on me; they would have never been called to the scene or, if called, they might not have come.

"Whose car is this?" the gray cop asked.

"Mine."

"Where's your license?"

"Free my hands and I'll get it for you."

"You're under arrest," he said, and was preparing to say more.

"What's the problem here?" a strong female voice inquired.

I was surprised to realize that tone had come from Marcia Pinkney.

She was wearing a brown housecoat and turquoise slippers. Her left hand clutched the housecoat at her breast and her right hand was held out to reiterate the question in case the officers were deaf — or dumb.

"Ma'am," Gray Cop said. "Is this your house?"

"Of course. Why do you have my daughter-in-law in chains?"

"Um," he said. "Daughter-in-law?"

"Answer my question, young man."

"We got a call from across the street that a black woman had broken into this house."

"And you were going to arrest her without even knocking on the door?"

"We had to secure her first. Um. Are you okay, ma'am?"

"Of course I am. Don't you see me?"

"Because we have her in custody. You don't have to be afraid."

"I'm not afraid of my daughter-in-law, Mrs. Theon Pinkney. She's the one who should be afraid. Four big men grabbing her and putting her in chains. What's wrong with you?"

The police stood there, slightly confused. I could see that they felt justified, even righteous, for grabbing me in Marcia's driveway. There was no question in their minds that I was a criminal and that they were on the side of the Law.

Marcia glanced at me then. We'd spent hours together but it was as if she hadn't really gotten a good look at me until seeing the tableau in her driveway.

"Take those chains from my daughter-in-law's arms," she said, sounding just a little like her son.

The gray cop hesitated. He didn't like being ordered around by a civilian. He was the one in charge. Maybe he considered arresting us both, but he knew that the witness across the street, the one who called about me, was probably still watching and that a patrol cop was subject to the same justice that he carried around on his shoulders like Superman's cape.

"Let her go," he muttered.

"But, Joe," the cop who tapped on my window said.

"Let her fuckin' go."

The first cop turned me around and took off the cuffs. I resisted rubbing my wrists — I didn't want to give them the satisfaction.

"I know there's something wrong here," Gray Cop said to Marcia. "And I will be back."

"There'll be no need for that, young man," Marcia said, looking up into the reflection in the policeman's shades. "Because what's wrong here is the same thing that's wrong with you. Just look in a mirror and you will see that like I see it now."

I went to the passenger's seat and popped the trunk again. I went to my big blue bag and pulled out my wallet.

"Do you still want to see my license?" I asked the senior cop.

"Let's get outta here," he said to his men.

They turned and walked to their cars, gave me a parting warning look, and drove out of the little cul-de-sac, so many angry crows humiliated at being chased by a little girl with a stick.

"Is it always like this?" Marcia asked me after the cops were gone.

"I haven't been out of my comfort zone for a long time, Marcia. Usually I'm in a place where everybody knows me and everybody treats me with respect. They might not mean it; they might not like me, but at least they smile and pretend."

Across the circle a white woman came out on the porch of her ranch-style home. She was tall and thin, wearing a burgundy robe decorated with a pattern that I couldn't make out from the distance.

"I don't understand what you mean," Marcia said.

"What just happened here is how people really feel," I said. "Your neighbor over there saw a black woman fooling around in the front yard and then go into your house. . . ."

"Old Nancy Bierny should mind her own business," Marcia said with venom.

"You would'a done the same thing, Marcia. If you saw a black woman goin' in and outta Nancy's at six in the morning, you would'a called the cops and said that someone was acting suspiciously in front of a neighbor's house. You would have been scared and the woman you saw would have been presumed guilty. That's the way it is in the straight world where the good folks live. That's part of the reason Theon left. He didn't want to be associated with the world you and your husband lived in — the world where he got beaten and you went to hide in another part of the house."

Marcia put a hand on my wrist.

"Please stop," she said. "I can't stand to think about it."

"Okay," I said. "Sorry. I left my number on the kitchen counter. If you want to come see Theon's body the night before, you just call. I got that cell phone on me all the time now."

Marcia pulled her hand away from my wrist and put it over her mouth. Maybe she didn't trust herself to speak.

I know if I were her that I wouldn't have known what to say.

There's a little shop on Robertson just north of Venice Boulevard. I'd not been inside before but whenever I drove past I thought that the kind of clothes they sold would be perfect for my mother. It was called Phyllis Designs.

I was thinking about that shop while at LeRoy's Chicken and Waffle House eating more calorie-rich food. I ate, wrote these words in my little journal, and reread a few chapters of *Kindred* by Octavia Butler. In between phrases I paused, thinking of the little dress shop.

Hours passed as I sat at the low wall of the outside patio, drinking coffee refills and turning from one project to the next. The waiter made me pay at one point. I suppose he thought I was some kind of thief who would try to get away without paying for the meal.

But that didn't bother me. I was thinking about Marcia and the gray cop, my father's gun and a new wardrobe for a new life.

"Can I help you?" asked a tall white woman in an orange one-piece dress.

The dress was designed for a woman younger than her fifty-something years but she probably looked better in it than she would in more age-appropriate garb.

She had brown hair and like-colored eyes and her teeth were too perfect to be her own. She was thin, almost skinny, and did yoga or Pilates daily, I was sure.

She wore little makeup and didn't give off the aura of sexuality. She strove to be attractive but kept the gate to her garden locked.

I had these thoughts because the woman was checking me out with the same intensity. She saw my fake breasts and tight body under the fat woman's yellow-and-blue dress. She saw my age and the disproportionate concentration of experience in my eyes. She saw also that my blue bag was a real Thimera, a ten-thousand-dollar accessory that could be purchased only at a single outlet on Rodeo Drive.

"I've always loved this shop when I drove by," I said. "So today I decided to come in."

The shop woman couldn't keep the hint of a sneer from her lips.

"Most of my clothes are for older women," she said. "A young girl like you has less to hide and more to be proud of."

"You're Phyllis?"

The excitement in my tone diminished the sourness on the designer's lips.

I understood Phyllis in that instant. She came from that very neighborhood, probably went to the high school across the street. She was a smart child and well-heeled. Phyllis didn't want to be just another housewife and was a generation or so too early to have been allowed into the world of high finance. So she decided to be an artist: a clothes designer. But try as she might the world of runways and fashion models was also beyond her. And so her husband . . . or maybe he divorced her for a younger partner, and so probably her parents bought her this shop. It was a hit among women of a certain age, women who wanted to show off but still had a little something to hide.

Phyllis's designs were craftier than the clothes made for New York and Parisian models. A thirty-three-year-old mother of two with fifteen extra pounds and less than perfect skin could don one of this shop's offerings and go to a church or temple fundraiser with confidence and even hints of beauty.

"It's just a small shop," Phyllis said, trying to figure out if she wanted me to leave or to sit and have coffee.

"My husband died a few days ago," I said.

"Oh, I'm sorry."

"Thank you," I said, casting my eyes around the small, clothes-crowded shop. "It was sudden and very sad, doubly so because we had grown apart and now we'll never be able to resolve those differences."

"What's your name?" the conflicted storeowner asked.

"Sandy. Sandy Peel, but my married name

was Pinkney."

"You speak so well," the older white woman said to the young black chick. "You must be well educated."

"No. When I was a little girl my father read to me and then, when I got older, he'd have me read to him for an hour every night. I think I must have combined the love for my father and reading and so, even though I dropped out before high school, I've always read hard books."

"Why'd you drop out?" my new potential best friend asked.

"After my father was murdered it was the only thing I could do."

"Murdered? Oh my God."

"In a way," I said, "what's happened with Theon, my husband, was the same as with my father. I cut my hair and threw away all my old clothes and my old life. And I'm here today to get new clothes to go along with my new life."

"What's that?" Phyllis asked. "What is your new life?"

"I really don't know, Phyllis. A lot of that has to do with you, I guess. I want to be something different."

"What are you now?" Phyllis Amber Schulman asked.

"I think," I said, "I think I'm a little lost."

"Why don't we sit and have some tea?"

"My husband and I lived a kind of wild life-style," I was saying to the clothes designer.

Phyllis had hung a Closed sign in the window of her shop, pulled the shade, and locked the door.

"Drugs?" she asked.

"Everything," I said. "I can't really go into details but we were way out there."

"And now that he's gone you see that there was something wrong with your life?"

"No," I said after a few moments honestly considering her question.

"Really?" Her question contained no value judgment. She seemed truly interested in who I was.

"I loved my friends and their lives before Theon died and I still do now that he's gone," I said. "It's just that I can see now that I have to move on. Do you know what I mean?"

"I used to have this boyfriend named Gary," she said. "He was a surfer and I was his girl, at least when we were in the same place. We did a lot of drinking and cocaine. I did things with him in the bed that I would never admit to.

"Gary loved me harder than either of my children, my husband, or my parents ever did. But . . ."

"What?" I put down my teacup and took this stranger's hand in mine.

"One day I woke up in this shack in Maui. Gary was unconscious from all the coke we snorted, and there were flies buzzing around the sink. I knew right then that Gary would never change and that I had to leave him or go down with him.

"I called my parents and they bought me a ticket. I didn't even leave Gary a note."

"Did you ever see him again?"

"When our friend Mike died," Phyllis said, nodding, "eight years later. We bumped into each other at the service. We just said hi and asked how each other was doing. We were both married with kids. He owned a surfboard shop. Still does."

"Did you feel like you made a mistake leaving him?" I asked. I really wanted to know.

Phyllis shook her head and looked at me with sad eyes. "No. We would have partied our way into early graves. But you know, I've never had anything in my life that felt as good as it did when I was with him. I sit in here sometimes talking to women just like me and I find myself wanting to hurry them out so I can call Gary up and beg him to come back. The only problem is that

163

there's no place to come back to."

I squeezed her hand.

"So you see, Sandy, I know what you're talking about."

I left with seven dresses, four skirts, two pant suits and two pairs of pants, nine blouses, various kinds of nonthong underpants, bras, hose, three pairs of low-heeled shoes, two hats, and a crazy wristwatch with a wide red band and garnet stones for the hours. The colors we chose were burgundy, dark gold, navy blue, lime, white, and tan. There were a few flower prints, and some pinstripes, but on the whole the colors were solid and uninteresting. They fit me well enough but the sizes were appropriate to my form. Phyllis held on to the BBW blue-and-yellow dress and the tattered tennis shoes to throw away. I left the store wearing a navy skirt and a shimmery (but far from vinyl) gold blouse. I wore no hose because it was a hot day, and my shoes were blue with hemp-corded wedge heels.

I hadn't felt sexier nor less attractive in years.

Phyllis saw me to the door and said goodbye. I nodded at her and she grabbed me in a passionate hug.

"I'm so happy that you came here to me,"

she said after reluctantly letting go.

"Really? Why?"

"Most of the time people come in here to hide something or to make themselves look better than they feel and to feel better than they look. They want to spend some money or talk about their husbands and boyfriends, their kids. I guess I kind of hate them. Here I am trying to make something, to create something, and you're the first customer I've ever had who wants to use my clothes the way I feel about them."

There were tears in her eyes. I allowed her to hug me again and then she kissed my cheek.

Phyllis made me feel normal. Her story about the debauched surfer and life outside the life she was supposed to live was really very close to my experience. She was a hint, an omen that there was a place for me somewhere else.

I had the big blue bag-holster open and on my lap as I pulled into the driveway of my huge, soulless home. There were no dangers, however, no men lying in wait.

I went straight to the kitchen table and began writing about my afternoon. Phyllis was very much on my mind. She was like a spider who had chosen her permanent corner and from there wove her webs. The crevice she lived in was somewhere in the Garden of Eden but she didn't realize that. Her talent was subtle but exquisite and the world would never know. I was a self-educated thinker but people in my world rarely realized it. And those who did resented me or wanted to fuck me in the rectum.

Phyllis and I were the same in some ways but that wasn't enough for us to be friends. Marcia Pinkney and I had in common an overwhelming pain but we could not really share it.

It seemed that on those small journal pages all I could do was describe a world of closed doors and failed dreams. Everything I was, everything I saw seemed to be its own opposite — why, I wrote, live in a world like that?

The phone rang while I was going over and over this pointless cycle of thought.

"Hello?"

"Deb?" a man said. He sounded as if he'd recently been crying.

"Hey, Jude. How are you?"

"I've been calling for two days."

"Oh. Sorry, I've been so busy. There's going to be a funeral next Saturday at Day's Rest. I hope you can come."

"Thank you," he said.

The value of death dawned upon me at that moment. People rarely meant so much with their words.

How are you?
I'm fine. You?
Getting along.
Great.

But when someone dies everyone has deep feelings that come to the surface, wailing and screaming and feeling profound.

Marcia and Mr. Dardanelle, even Lieutenant Mendelson showed sincere deference to me and to my dead.

"Can I do anything for you, Deb?" Jude asked.

"I don't think so, honey. Either everything is done or it's already too late."

Jude gasped through the line and I felt sorry for him.

"Was he . . . was he in a lot of pain?" the eternal friend asked.

"No. It was quick, and if I know Theon he was having a very good time before he passed."

"An accident?"

"A video camera that was plugged into the wall fell in the bathtub."

"Oh my God."

He sounded so sweet. I wondered how

such a mild-mannered man could be con-
strued as dangerous.

Jude was much smarter than Theon. He
was also quite knowledgeable. Whenever the
three of us got together Theon would get
pissed because Jude was happy discussing
D. H. Lawrence or Virginia Woolf with me.
He had a college education and his mind
moved easily between speculation and substance.

Jude understood what a video camera in
the bathtub meant. His silence was another
kind of respect. His friendship, though not
for me, not exactly, was just the thing I
needed.

"Would you like to meet for dinner?" I
asked him.

"Tonight?"

"Uh-huh."

"Where?"

When I got to Monarc's Jude was already at
a small round table in a partially secluded
corner. He stood to kiss my cheeks and
press my hands. His trousers were black,
shirt gray — he even wore a black beret
centered on his head like proper French-
men wear them.

"You changed your hair and your clothes,"
he said.

"You mean I don't look like a cheap whore anymore."

"You always had class, Deb. Even on the worst days you rose above the . . . the shit."

Jude was a small man. His hairline was receding but he wasn't yet forty.

"He loved you," Jude said.

"As well as he could. He loved you too."

I luxuriated in the pleasure Jude took in this secondhand emotion. Tears formed in his eyes and I was absolutely sure that no one in the world would miss Theon more than that little man.

"Sometimes I used to hate you, Debbie," he confessed. "You know, I wanted to be going home with him but he wanted you. You."

I didn't know what to say. Jude's ardor was uncontainable. Theon's stupid uncalculated suicide brought out feelings from every corner and depth.

"But you were always nice to me," Jude said. "And I'd go home feeling so guilty because you never treated me bad.

"But he loved you. . . . He told me that you were the woman made for him. It wasn't just sex either. He said that you were his soul mate. And, and, and I don't know. In some ways it broke my heart but made me happy at the same time."

I noticed Rash Vineland staring at us from three tables away. For some reason the sight of him made me reach across the table and take Jude's hand.

"We both had a place in his life, honey," I said. "You were one of his only real friends. I mean, he had a lot of acquaintances but when something was important he always called you."

The gratitude in Jude's eyes was replaced by something that seemed like guilt. I thought at the time that he was feeling ashamed for his jealousy.

He squeezed my hand and the waiter came up with our menus.

"I can't stay, Deb," Jude said. "Right after I talked to you I got this call. I have to go meet with the F-Troop Theatre Company. I'm designing the sets and costumes for their new show."

"Oh. You should invite me when it goes up."

"I'll be happy to. I'll have them send an invitation to your house for the opening."

"Um . . . maybe you should do it by e-mail," I said. "You have my dot-com address, don't you?"

"What's wrong, Deb? Why can't they send it to your house?" The joy of Jude was his laserlike perceptivity.

"Theon wasn't the best businessman, hon. He had us in hock up to his nuts. I don't think I'll be in that house very long."

"Didn't he have a life insurance policy?"

The sound that came out of me was rarer than any orgasm or breakdown. It was so odd . . . my laughter: high and punctuated, surging up from my diaphragm like some kind of pent-up explosion finally finding its exit.

I leaned over the table and I think Jude was a little frightened. My whole body shook with a mirth that was both light and dark. I lowered my head into cupped hands. It must have looked like I was crying. All I could do was imagine Theon Pinkney, known to the world as Axel Rod, having the wherewithal to plan for something like death, to worry about what he left behind him in the trail of wreckage that was his journey through life. I conjured up the image of the big-bellied man with the lovely naked child at his side, looking like some minor Greek god of the sea emerging with an errant nymph who caught his fancy.

Gods didn't buy life insurance policies, didn't worry about money in the bank. Gods were eternal icons of fecundity and desire.

171

"It's gonna be all right, Deb," Jude was saying.

I raised my head, intending to assure Jude that I was laughing — not crying. But there were tears of hilarity in my eyes and I couldn't speak because I knew that I'd start laughing again. So I nodded and held out my hands to him.

Jude stared at me with intensity. He was worried, inspecting my emotions with deep concentration.

"I really have to go," he said apologetically.

"It's okay, Jude. I'm going to stay and have some soup, I think."

I could see Rash casting glances in our direction.

"Are you sure you'll be okay?"

I was trying not to laugh, to bury the silly feeling I had about Theon and the future.

"I'm fine, Jude. Better than I can really say right now. It was so sweet of you to call, and . . . and when I finally make the plans for the service I'd love it if you would say a few words about Theon."

Jude was shocked by this request. He started and then sat back.

"You mean you want me to come up to the podium?"

"You can't do it from the pews."

"I, I, I haven't . . . I mean, Theon never really included me in his public life."

"But you were his friend and you both need this good-bye."

"I have to go, Deb," he said. "I have to go."

He lurched up from the table and staggered to the door. His gait was so odd and pronounced that the waiters and bartender watched warily.

When Jude was gone I wondered about the information that passed between us. He was thinking things that I had no idea of and I was experiencing emotions that he could not understand. Still, we seemed to have shared a profound moment. I couldn't remember the last time anyone had made me laugh out loud. It might have been my father, long before he was murdered and I became a whore.

The laughter made me hungry. I ordered veal with escarole and saffron rice. I had a glass of dark red wine that the waiter gave me without naming a vintage. He just said, "I have something I think you'll like," and I nodded.

For some time I ate without looking at Rash Vineland. There was a smile on my face and a new world somewhere in the recesses of my mind. The substance around me felt malleable. It wasn't that I felt comfortable or secure. My dense pubic hair was growing in and I'd crossed a big director in the industry; my husband was dead and I had been pushed past broke into serious debt. But the veal was excellent and I could bring joy into people's lives without spreading my ass for their inspection and titillation.

"Salad, madam?" the waiter asked while clearing away the dinner dishes.

"Please."

I turned my attention to Rash and crooked a finger. He got right up and strode the six paces to my table.

"Was that your husband?" he asked while pulling out the chair that Jude had vacated.

"And how are you this evening, Rash?" I replied.

"Uh, okay, fine. How are you?"

I smiled and the waiter brought my salad.

"I like this dress," he said.

I was wearing a white sundress that didn't crowd my tits or ass. It accented my figure simply because it fit and I liked the way it made me look — somewhat older and a few pounds over the limit.

"Thank you."

Rash wanted to speak but didn't know

what to say. His discomfort tickled me. He was shy but not because of the size of my nipples or the sighs I lied with on the screen. He wanted to make conversation, to carve out a place where he and I could communicate — one way or another. His wants were commonplace and predictable, like the plot of children's cartoons on PBS. The story was safe, nonviolent, and fully dressed.

"The man I was sitting with is a friend of the family," I said. "My husband died a few days ago and Jude was offering his condolences."

"Oh."

"It was terrible," I said, agreeing with Rash's unspoken sympathy. "A terrible accident. I've been a little thrown off and Jude, who was a good friend of Theon's, was offering his help."

"Theon was your husband's name?"

I nodded.

"I'm really sorry. I can leave you alone if you want."

"No," I said. "I don't want to be alone. I mean I can be if necessary but you're nice. You know how to have a conversation."

"You wouldn't know it by the way my foot's in my mouth right now."

"That's my fault. I'm a little tricky when it comes to talking to men. I like to keep 'em a little off balance. Otherwise most guys want to walk all over you."

I stared directly into the café au lait-colored young man's eyes. It was all he could do not to avert his gaze.

"I hardly know what to say when somebody experiences a loss like yours," he said with barely a stutter. "Nobody close to me has ever died."

"You're lucky. It hurts when they're gone. And it doesn't matter if it's slow or fast, whether it's a long drawn-out disease or an unexpected accident. When they're gone the world turns upside down and you're left holding on, trying not to fall off."

Rash gave me a little half smile, as if he were experiencing pain. I reached over and laid my hand on his.

"You wanna come over to my house for a while?" I asked him. "We could just sit and talk. I'd really like that."

We took separate cars.

Rash followed my taillights east and then over the mountain into Pasadena. When we got to my house on South Elm I parked on the street and he pulled up behind.

I waited by the passenger's side for him.

"Nice car," he said. "Nice house."

"Are you a gigolo?" I asked.

"Why would you ask something like that?"

"You're talking about the worth of my possessions," I said, feeling as if I were, once again, following a bad script. "So are you?"

"Not hardly."

"What do you do for a living?"

He was thrown off, I thought, not so much by the question but the fact of my asking it on the street — before we went into the house.

"Um . . . I'm an architect."

"You design skyscrapers and stuff like that?"

"Not so much. Mostly houses, usually interiors. You know, rooms and maybe a patio or two. When people are designing or redesigning their homes I sit with them and work out the possibilities. After that I draw up plans and maybe help them find contractors."

"How's that doing?"

"On and off. I pay my rent most months. I owe money here and there, but I got this job for the interiors of this new office building going up on Wilshire. That'll see me through to the end of next year."

There were stars in the sky behind the modest architect. For a moment I was distracted by them.

"You wanna go in?" Rash asked.

"That's why we're here, right?"

"Maybe you changed your mind now that you know I'm a poor architect."

"Your job is the last thing I'm worried about, honey; believe me."

Rash smiled and I took him by the arm.

We were halfway up the stone pathway when someone said, "Excuse me, Ms. Dare."

A white man in an upscale white trench coat was approaching from across the street. He was of normal height and build but something about the way he walked gave a sense of confidence, even finality. He was familiar-looking — but I'd met so many people that he was to me more a type than an actual person with a name to be remembered.

"Yes?" I said.

He strode right up to us and for an instant I believed that we, Rash and I, were both dead.

"It is you, isn't it?" the white man asked. "I mean, the last time I saw you your hair was longer and a different color."

"Do I know you?"

"Obviously not. But it is you, isn't it?"

"It's me, Mr. . . . ?"

"Manetti. Coco Manetti. I called you."

The evening was suddenly something different than I imagined. Now, before I could practice normal conversation with a regular guy, I'd have to survive the machinations of a self-made gangster.

"I'm sorry, Mr. Manetti. I've been getting hundreds of calls, literally. I've been upset."

"I can see that," he said, glancing at Rash.

"This is my friend Tom Vance," I lied. "He's helping me plan the funeral."

"I knew your husband," Coco said.

"He's mentioned you. Something about having to work off a debt."

Manetti's cold eyes watched Rash's face for a moment and then he turned back to me.

"Can I come in for a few minutes before you start . . . planning?" he asked.

I led both men into the white-on-white-in-white living room. Rash looked confused but he didn't say anything to contradict the lie I'd created for him. Coco went to the long sofa and sat down in the exact center.

I considered offering my guests drinks but decided against it, because I didn't want to leave them alone together.

In the electric light Coco had eyes that were dark brown. His skin was the color — and had the pallor — of death. Under the trench coat he had on gray wool trousers

179

and a lime golf shirt. His shoes were real snakeskin and he wore no socks.

"I'll make this quick," Coco said as he leaned forward, placing his elbows on his knees. "You know Richard Ness?"

"Sure, I know Dick."

Coco smiled.

"Dick," he said, "yes. Dick sold me Theon's marker. It is now to me that you owe his debt."

In spite of his ominous meaning I was impressed with his sentence structure.

"Oh. I see."

"For some reason Dick was worried that he wouldn't get satisfaction in the deal with you and so I paid him eighty cents on the dollar, knowing that I'd have better luck."

"You can't squeeze blood from a stone, Mr. Manetti."

"You'd be surprised the blood I've seen."

"Theon never told me about this debt," I explained. "I haven't signed a thing. And he left me with nothing. The bank owns this house and his car, all our accounts are empty, and the credit cards are as kissing close to being maxed out as you can get."

"None of that's a problem," Coco said, sitting back and waving his hand carelessly. "The last time Theon was in hock to me he just worked off the debt — like you said."

I could feel the hardness come into my face.

"You could come work for a friend of mine," Manetti continued. "Two or three months of hard work and we'd be clear. Six months and you'll be able to climb out of debt."

"I don't do that anymore," I said. The words felt good in my mouth. My nostrils flared.

"That might be a mistake."

"Listen, man," I said. "My husband just died. My accountants tell me that I'll be thrown out in the street soon. I have to bury Theon and catch my breath."

"When's the funeral?"

"Saturday at two forty-five."

"Where?"

"Day's Rest." I could have lied but that wouldn't have put Manetti off the scent.

Coco got to his feet slowly and yet lithely. "I'll be there. If Theon told you about our little deal you know that I mean serious business. I'm not like Dick at all."

With that Coco Manetti walked toward the front door and let himself out. I followed him and switched on the alarm system.

"What was that all about?" Rash asked. He had trailed behind me.

"You can leave if you want," I said, push-

181

ing my way past him, headed for the kitchen.

Rash came after me, which I both liked and dreaded. I was still in the lead when we arrived at the kitchen.

I turned on the lights.

"So who was he?" Rash asked while I peered into the double-doored refrigerator.

"You want some banana-orange-strawberry juice?"

"I think I could use a real drink," he said.

"In the low cabinet behind you."

Rash squatted down while I poured my juice. Then I went to the little alcove next to the dark windows.

"Can I have some of this brandy?" he asked.

"Sure. The glasses are over your head. You need ice?"

"No, thanks."

I watched him pour a triple shot into a squat glass. He seemed to be quivering a little.

I didn't blame him.

He pulled in across from me.

"So?" He managed a light tone and I was impressed.

"My husband died in debt," I said. "Some of the people he owed money to are what you might call disreputable. This guy Dick was a kind of leg breaker. Manetti is somewhat worse than that."

"Should we call the police?"

"And say what?"

Instead of answering he took a healthy swig of our thirty-year-old cognac. Rash was wearing a buff-colored jacket, blue jeans, black tennis shoes, and a white T-shirt. Only in California could you find black people like him and me.

"What kind of work did he want you to do?"

"Do you want to be my friend, Rash?" I decided to speak without thinking, to find out what was going on in a kind of trance-like stream of consciousness. If Rash could flow with that then he could come along — wherever it was I was headed.

"I don't know you well enough to answer that question yet."

"Do you think that you might like to be my friend?"

"That's why I'm here. Though I'm not quite sure what I'm getting into."

Rash was smiling. He had a small gap between his two upper front teeth. He was looking straight at me without the slightest aggression.

"Are you gay, Rash?"

"No. Why?"

"Why does a girl ask a guy if he's gay?"

"Uh . . ."

I had been in the business for too long. I was blocking the sex scene that this conversation would become on Linda Love's or Roger Bonair's set. The shy guy and the brash whore. He's her husband's clueless friend and she's hungry for sexual exploration. . . .

"Rash is a funny name for such a shy guy," I said, trying to derail my knee-jerk train of thought.

"Yeah," he said. "Yep."

He looked around the room and I saw that I was losing him.

"Are you looking for a way out of here, Rash?"

"So that guy, that Coco, he was like a gangster?"

"I wouldn't be upset if this was too much for you."

"I just want to know what happened with that guy. Why didn't you tell him my real name?"

"I told you," I said, trying to keep the frustration out of my voice, "my husband died but he was in debt. Theon had a lot of vices. He gambled and chased women; he liked to drink good brandy too. Guys like that often show up on people like Manetti's radar. I didn't tell him your name because

184

you are none of his business."

Whenever Rash crinkled up his face, trying to understand what was being said, I had the urge to kiss him. I managed not to give in to these frequent urges.

"And what about you?" the coffee-and-cream-colored young architect asked.

"What about me?" I stood up from the table, reminding myself of Mary Astor in *The Maltese Falcon.*

"That gangster wanted you to go to work for him."

I considered lying and, in a flash, I understood the femme fatale of film noir and noir novels. They lied because it was easier than the truth, because they had been invited in for their charms and lies, because the truth always sounded so guilty when they were just trying to make it through the day — like everybody else.

I tried to say something but the words weren't there.

I took in a deep breath to compose myself.

"You don't have to tell me if you don't want to," Rash said.

For some reason the idea of love crossed my mind. It seemed to me then, in spite of the triteness, that love was an impossible goal unless you broke it down into pieces — fragments. I could love my father because he was tall and strong and funny, because he read stories to me and understood how the world worked. He loved me because I was small and needed him. Those two loves came together but they were not one love.

"Do you want me to leave?" Rash asked.

I looked at him, feeling that he was alien, like a high school foreign-exchange student from a country that no one in the class, not even the teacher, had ever heard of. Some kid who wore strange, dull-colored clothing and smelled like bread.

"What?" he said.

"You want something to eat?" I managed to ask.

"I'm still full from the restaurant."

"Oh . . . right," I said. "I forgot about that."

"Why did that guy call you Ms. Dare?"

"Dare is my stage name."

"You act?"

"Oh yeah."

"Theater?"

"If you're looking for an excuse all you have to do is walk out to your car."

"Why won't you talk to me, Sandra?"

"I am talking."

"I ask you if you work in theater and you tell me that I can leave. That's not talking."

I grinned at that, appreciating the young

architect's ability to stay on the scent.

"How many nights have you eaten at Monarc's since we met there?" I asked.

"Every night."

"Why?"

"In case you came in." He looked down at my hands.

"Kinda like stalking somebody who isn't there."

"I liked talking to you."

"But you don't like it now," I countered.

"Yes, I do. I'd rather talk to you than anyone else I know."

"Isn't that kind of obsessive?"

"No," he insisted. "It's just sudden."

"Do you have a girlfriend?"

He hesitated.

"Come on now, honey," I said. "Tell me the truth."

"Yeah."

"What's her name?"

"Annabella. Annabella Atoll."

"Are you engaged?"

"No."

"Do you live together?" I had almost forgotten Coco Manetti by then.

"Uh-uh, no. We . . . we date."

"And where has Annabella been all these nights you were waiting for me?"

"She goes to grad school at UCLA. She's

studying for her accounting finals. I won't see her for at least another ten days."

He was a nice guy but a little out of focus, like somebody you meet at a bar after the sixth or seventh drink — the kind of man I'd remember liking but just couldn't recall the name of. I had been blaming this haziness on my depressive trauma, but just then I saw that it was Rash himself that was out of alignment in the world he lived in.

"Do you recognize me?" I asked.

"You mean from TV or something?"

"Answer the question."

He scrunched up his face and concentrated. After thirty seconds or so he shook his head no. He'd have to be a consummate liar to have succeeded with an act like that.

"My husband just died," I said, lifting the words up like a shield.

"I'm not trying to do anything," he said. "I mean, I was, I am attracted to you, but I wouldn't have even said anything in the restaurant if you didn't want me to. And I came here because you asked me."

"Kind of like a puppet." I immediately regretted these words. I had been playing the hardhearted seductress for so long that the role was both my first and last resort.

Rash moved his head from side to side, genuflected in the chair as if he meant to rise and walk away, but then sat back.

"You just looked so calm," he said at last. "Sitting there reading your book, looking up now and then with this little smile you got. I don't know . . . I guess I wanted to feel like that."

"Like what exactly?"

"Like I wasn't all the time waiting for something else to happen. Like I was just sitting in a chair completely comfortable with myself."

"You were," I said.

"No," Rash Vineland said.

He looked me directly in the eye. That's what I was waiting for: for a man who had not seen or heard about my genitals who was talking straight in my face.

"Get up," I commanded. "Come with me."

I took him by the hand and led him back into the polar bear room. I sat him on the large sofa facing a fake fireplace and picked up a nacre-plated remote-control unit.

"My full stage name is Debbie Dare," I said. "Have you ever heard that name?"

"I don't think so."

"Is Annabella pretty?"

"Yeah, I guess."

"Very pretty?"

He nodded.

189

"Why did you start talking to me at the restaurant?" I asked him. "I mean, I wasn't wearing any makeup and my dress looked like it came from a Salvation Army box."

"I already told you. It was the way you looked out," he said, "like you were really seeing something. When I saw you I wanted to know what you were thinking, who you were."

"And what about now?"

He stared for a moment and then nodded.

I smiled.

"It's not going to be easy getting to know me, Rash Vineland," I said. "Annabella won't like you being my friend and the friendship will be hard on you."

He took in a deep breath through his nose and then exhaled through his mouth.

"The one thing that'll be easy for you to do is walk away," I continued. "You can walk out of my life right now or next week and I won't complain."

"Why do you sound so hard?"

"That's the way I am. Can you accept that?"

"I'm here right now."

"Fine. Now . . . before you can know who I am and what kind of friend I'll be, you have to know who I was."

190

I pressed a button on the fancy remote and the oil painting of white horses prancing in a pale golden field slid away, revealing a seventy-two-inch plasma screen. I hit a few more keys and a DVD hidden in another part of the house began to play.

The title of the Crux Brothers film *Debbie Does Death* appeared and Rash's mouth fell open.

"Have you seen it?" I asked.

He shook his head.

The film began with tiny clips of me getting fucked in a dozen different ways. My heart was racing with panic but I made myself stay there and watch.

The story started with a carjacking. Debbie and her husband park at a rest stop because they're so much in love that they can't wait to get home to have sex. Hooded men attack them, kill the nameless husband, and drag me off to a sinister mansion, where they and a dozen more men with hoods perform extraordinary sexual acts on me. At one point four different men were inside me, getting off on one another as much as with me. I remembered somewhere in the middle of the film how Joey Crux had brought three ounces of cocaine to the set so that my inhibitions were all but non-existent.

Maybe half an hour into the film, just before I was to walk into a door that had the name "Mr. Death" stenciled on it, I pressed the off button and the plasma screen went black.

This didn't stop Rash from staring though. He was looking at the blank screen with the same intensity that he watched the flabby, ass-slapping story.

"Is your dick hard, Rash?"

"Very."

"I'm not that woman anymore."

"I can see that. Why'd you want me to see it if you don't do that anymore?"

"Because I want to know if I can make a transition from what you just saw to the world you live in without lying and hiding my past."

"Are you embarrassed about making that movie?"

"I've been in hundreds of films like that and I'm not ashamed of anything I've done or anybody I've known."

"So are you quitting because your husband died? Was he the one who made you do . . . that?"

"No, not really," I said. "He opened the door but I went through under my own steam. I mean, there are reasons I became what you saw up there but I didn't have to do it. I wasn't a sex slave or anything like that.

"I don't even know if I'm quitting because Theon died. Something happened to me before I ever got home that day. I felt what it was like to die and be reborn —"

"Like a Christian?"

"No. Not religion. It was something else, something inside me that I didn't want to see but suddenly I couldn't look away. Not even that. It was me all of a sudden realizing what it was that I saw, like for the last sixteen years I had been seeing the world one way and then, for no reason whatever, things looked different."

"I think it was good that you showed me that, that film," Rash Vineland said.

"Why?"

"Because if you just told me I wouldn't have understood. I mean, I would have thought I did, but really I had to see it with you sitting there to know what was and what wasn't."

We sat there next to each other in the bright white room, lost in our own thoughts about reality and truth. The flesh around Rash's eyes crinkled with the attempt to understand but I was dead set on not kissing him — or any other man.

"Do you want to spend the night?" I asked him.

Again he hesitated. This time I smiled.

"We're not going to have sex," I assured him. "And it's not because you have a girlfriend. I just want to have some friendship from someone who doesn't fuck or fight for a living."

"Do you, um, usually sleep with your friends?"

"Tonight I am."

After showing my nervous new friend to the bedroom I went to the bathroom, where Theon died, took off my dress, and put on a cream-colored slip. Rash had stripped down to his boxers while I was gone. I could see the erection straining against the fabric.

"Across the hall is a guest bedroom," I said. "If you have to come you can go over there and do what you need to do. We have a cleaning lady, at least for a little while longer, so you don't have to straighten up."

"Maybe, maybe I'll go over there for a little while right now," he said.

After he was gone I turned off all the lights except for the reading lamp. I went to Theon's night table and rummaged around until I located the one book he had always intended to read but never did, *The Twelve*

Caesars, the ancient text about the private and public lives of some of the most powerful men in history.

Theon had that book as a kind of counterbalance to my ever-changing library, but it was more than that. Theon saw himself as some kind of working royalty. He was king of the fuck flicks in the old days when he made a movie every week. Even after his star waned and he began living off my money and fame he acted as if everything centered around him. The historical work was a kind of talisman for his ego.

I decided to read it for him as an offering to his death.

I had just settled in and opened the book to the preface when Rash came back into the bedroom.

"That was quick," I said.

"I don't usually watch films like that. My parents thought they were trash and every girlfriend I ever had was too proper to want to see one."

"You could have watched it with some guys," I suggested, putting *The Twelve Caesars* to rest on the night table.

"I get nervous around guys even when they're just talking about sex," he said as he got under the covers.

I cut off the light and turned my back to

195

him. For a long while he lay behind me, motionless.

"Hold me, Rash."

He curled up behind me, managing to get his arm around me without caressing my breasts. He exhaled with some strength and then did so again. After that his breathing was normal — for a while.

"I have a son," I said.

"How old is he?"

"Five. He'll be six in December."

"Where is he?"

"At my stepsister's house."

"While you go through this funeral stuff?"

"No. He lives with her. My brother Cornell was trying to find me unfit to raise a child when I was pregnant and so Delilah took Edison in."

"Edison's a nice name."

Rash managed to say just the right thing even though he wasn't trying.

"It's my father's brother's name. He raised my father and one time, when I was a little girl talking about when I grew up and became a mom, my dad said that the only thing he wanted was if I had a son that I'd name him Edison after my dead uncle."

"That's the perfect way to honor your father," Rash said, and I pulled his arms up to my breast.

For a moment he held his breath.

"Um," he said.

"Yes?"

"Why aren't we having sex?"

"I'm not," I said. "You have the room across the hall."

"Uh, okay, but why aren't you?"

"In the last four weeks I've had unprotected sex with at least sixteen men and almost as many women. We all have regular checkups and most of us are professional enough not to work if we think we're sick. But I won't know about my health for sure until at least nine months from my last sexual encounter.

"And even if that wasn't true, you have to know that sex to me is like cornflakes or toothpaste. I don't connect it with love or even mild concern. I don't anticipate sex; I dread it.

"That's why I brought you to bed."

"Why?"

"Because you're sweet and considerate and I knew from the first minute we talked that you would keep it in your pants and hold me anyway."

"Um, you know, I think I have to go in the other room for a while again. I'll be back."

I started counting when Rash got up from

the bed. I made it to seventy-eight before he returned and embraced me again.

I could feel his heart thundering against my back.

This made me smile.

"Why?" I whispered.

"Why what?" His voice was husky and deep.

"Why are you staying with me?"

"Because ever since I met you I wanted to see you again. But I thought that you would just smile maybe or say hi. I was hoping that if you came in, you wouldn't walk out after seeing me, and I hoped you'd let me sit at your table."

I hummed and hugged his hand to my cheek.

"Why do you want me to stay with you?" he asked.

"I told you already . . . because I want a man to hold me and to hold back at the same time," I said.

"And you expect this man to hold back for nine months?"

"At least."

He let go of me then and got out of bed.

"Are you leaving?" the girl inside me asked.

"Just goin' across the hall for a bit."

■ ■ ■ ■

He made two more trips to the guest bedroom in the night. I woke up each time he left but fell back to sleep almost immediately. Each time he returned he held me tighter, with more conviction. And each time I felt more and more centered in myself.

When I awoke in the morning we were sleeping across the bed from each other. I leaned over him and tickled the tip of his nose until he opened his eyes.

I felt fresh and happy; he looked like he hadn't slept at all.

"This friendship really is gonna be too hard on you, huh, Rash Vineland?" I opined.

"No."

That was the first moment of real fear that I'd felt in what seemed like years. It was as if Rash had reached into my chest and grabbed hold of my insides.

"What's wrong?" he asked.

"Nothing. I have to go somewhere."

"Can I come?"

"No. I have to put on some clothes."

"Can I watch?"

"No," I said playfully. "Go out to the kitchen and make us some breakfast."

Rash could cook. He made cheese omelets and bacon with home fries seasoned with onions, bell peppers, and jalapeños. He even made coffee and served me banana-orange-strawberry juice.

"What would Annabella say about all this?" I asked after he served the meal.

Almost immediately I regretted the question. Rash's face scrunched up and his mouth twisted as if he'd eaten something bitter.

"I can't worry about that," he said. "I mean, the way I think about it is, how'd I feel if she did that? But it's not just the doing."

"No?"

"Uh-uh. The problem is if some guy made her feel the way you do me."

"How do I make you feel?" I asked, thinking, *Shut up, girl.*

"Like I was floating out in the middle of the ocean," he said. "Like I could rise up in the sky like evaporation. I mean, it doesn't make any sense but there it is."

"It's Sunday," I said. "People have those feelings on Sundays."

Rash grinned and nodded.

I knew that I had gone too far with him even without having sex.

"Should we stop this now?" I asked.

He got that look again, the one he had the first time in the restaurant when I told him I had to leave.

"I don't want to stop," he said.

"It might cost you."

"What am I saving for if not for this?"

"I have your number in my purse," I said, thinking that there was also a loaded gun in there. "I'll call tonight."

"Can I have your number too?"

I scribbled it down for him and tore the leaf out of my journal.

He got up and walked to the doorway, then stopped and walked all the way back to kiss my cheek. I didn't kiss him. I knew better.

Rock of Ages House of Worship had grown since I was a little girl. When I was small the church was too: a little mauve-colored bungalow on a big lot at the dead end of a small downtown block. Now it was a stone fortress standing as high as a five-story building, with three thousand seats and twice that many active members. The parking lot was protected by high fences. The driveway had three uniformed guards.

They let my Jaguar into the lot. The chief security man pointed me to one of the few open parking spaces.

I made my way down a flagstone path to the side door of the church. Music was already playing, a huge choir was singing "Jericho," and the assembled worshipers were on their feet singing along. There were huge stained-glass windows installed side by side down both walls, and a high platform where the choir sang, and an even higher dais where the preacher would give his sermon.

I was wearing a dark blue dress that came down to my calves and slightly lighter blue medium-heeled shoes. My wide-brimmed straw hat was of a fine weave and white in color. I carried a maroon handbag and wore aqua calfskin gloves that I had taken home from a movie I'd made.

I stood in the back looking around the assembled congregation, listening to the music, trying to feel like I belonged.

On the right side of the auditorium I first recognized Newland, my younger brother. He was standing next to my mom. On her other side was Cornell and past him a woman I didn't recognize. Behind them was my father's adopted daughter by an earlier marriage — Delilah — and next to her, singing his heart out, was Edison, my son.

I would have known Eddie if he was a full-grown man, but I only ever saw him on holidays, when I wasn't working.

I made my way over to the Peel clan. I reached past an Asian woman standing on the aisle and touched Newland's shoulder while the room cried out in praise-song. Looking at me, uncomprehending at first, Newland's smile of recognition was a memory that I'd hold dear for the rest of my life.

He whispered something to the small Asian woman and she came out in the aisle, signaling with her hands for me to take her place.

I moved next to Newland and he gave me a one-armed hug.

"Sandy," he said in my ear. "Mom'll be so happy you're here."

I glanced at the profile of my mother, who hadn't seen me yet, and saw over her shoulder Cornell's face. He was lighter skinned than Newland and I and of a heavy build. There was some hair on his chin, but not quite a beard, and a scowl for me that had not changed since the first time the police brought me home and my mother spent the night crying.

The song was nearing its high point. I

could hear Edison's singing in my ears. I closed my eyes and girded myself for the fights and recriminations, for the forgiveness and the loss that would not be dispelled by my brief return.

The singing was over and we all sat looking up at the seated choir hovered over by the empty sky-blue pulpit.

The gospel group's robes were dark red with cream lapels that went all the way down the front. They sat with military precision, waiting for the next movement in the Lord's day.

Cornell was staring at me.

My mother realized this and looked my way. Her smile was immediate and she gave me a little wave. She inhaled through her nostrils and held that breath for three or four beats.

I looked away and toward the front of the church. A small woman in ministerial black was making her way, rather inelegantly, up to the platform.

She reminded me of a bug trying to negotiate an unfamiliar vertical climb.

Finally she made it to the podium.

"Good Sunday, brothers and sisters," she said in a voice that was multitoned, like a jazz trumpet in the hands of a master.

"Good Sunday," two thousand or more

throats murmured and declared.

"I want to thank Brother Elbert and his lovely choir for their singing and Sister Eloise for her organ and this congregation for your voices raised in song and devotion."

A tremor seemed to go through the audience, a kind of collective hum of satisfaction.

"I know there are many of you out there who come to church each week because you know I don't mess around. . . ."

Laughter.

"I don't love the sound of my own voice and I don't waste time telling you what you already know. I don't need to tell ya that if you lied this week, or if you cheated someone, that you sinned. You know if you sinned. You know if you did wrong. You don't need a minister for that."

"Teach," someone cried out.

"You don't need a minister to follow you to the den of iniquity and tell you that you shouldn't be there. You don't need me to see you beat your children or your spouse in order for you to know that you did wrong. When you use the Lord's name in vain you got ears to hear it. And when you turn your back to suffering it's not my job to point and say, 'Look there.' "

The minister opened her eyes so wide that

I could appreciate it from my seat.

"No. That's not my job," she continued. "You've all been to church before. You've heard all, or nearly all, the stories in the Bible. You know about Sodom and Gomorrah, Adam and Eve, Cain and Abel, Babylon, the pharaohs, Moses, Abraham, and our savior on the cross. You know. I don't have to tell ya about Noah's ark navigating the great flood, or John the Baptist. I don't have to talk about Judas's role at the Last Supper or quote some verse you might not yet have heard. There's a Bible you can read for yourself in a forgotten drawer in your house. . . ."

More laughter. Even I smiled. I still had my childhood white leather-bound testaments in a drawer at home.

"You can turn the page just as easily as I can. You can get down on your knees without me askin' it. I'm not here to tell you stories of long ago and far away. I'm not here to point out sin and throw stones. I got my own sins to atone for. I got my own glass house."

"Amen," a woman cried.

"Preach," a fellow parishioner replied.

"I'm tellin' you," the minister said. "I'm tellin' you here and now that this pulpit does not raise me up above you. It doesn't make me smarter or better, not one whit closer to God. We are all in the same soup down here. And every day we have to reach out" — she raised her arms above her head — "and try to touch Him and feel Him and love Him and most of all we have to do His work."

The lady minister looked around the silent room. She had us all at that moment.

She was an older woman. Her skin was the brown of an overripe melon. Her face was clear of worry.

"I'm not gonna preach old stories that you've heard a thousand times," she said. "That kind of preachin' is for the children who are just now learnin' the path up . . . and the road down.

"What I'm talkin' about is you and me and what we might do to make this world something that reflects the teachings of all the great prophets."

She stopped again and rubbed her nose with the fingers of her left hand.

"Ruby Jenkins," she said. "Does anybody out there know Ruby?"

She looked around but no one replied.

"Ruby Jenkins," the preacher intoned. "She lives six and a half blocks from this church. Ruby has an illegal room at the back of a commercial property. She also has a fever and infected sores on her feet and back. I hear that she's from Tennessee and her family has moved on from these parts. She's an old woman but she looks older and she feels pain every day. She don't sleep and she cain't walk because of her fever and her feet. She cain't come to God and I believe that God is wondering why no one goes to her. Because you know God does not reside in this house. The omnipotent spirit is not prisoner on Sundays to us in our best clothes and on our best behavior."

The minister — I never learned her name — looked around the room telling us with her silence to consider her words.

"No," she continued after that exquisite quietude, "God is not ours. We belong to Him. We are here to do His work. His home is in that back room with Ruby and in the jail cell with some'a your sons and daughters and their friends. He might not even be here today. Your prayers might be on the back burners, in a saved file like in some giant computer. God might not get to readin' your prayers for a thousand years because He is worried about suffering and the pain that we ignore in this fine house we've built.

"But you have to understand, brothers and sisters, that this building looks beautiful in your eyes but it's no more than Ruby

208

Jenkins's room in the eyes of the Lord. You come here to plan your baptisms and say your prayers, to hear stale Bible stories and compare hats. But out there" — the minister pointed to her left — "out there is the real cathedral. This earth is God's palace and real prayer is the succor of sufferin' in His name.

"Ruby Jenkins is one in ten thousand lost and ailing, ten million. There are hungry children and drunken men, women sellin' their bodies and wise men plannin' the murders of millions callin' themselves God-fearing and thinkin' about sainthood.

"Prayer for us, brothers and sisters, is not the childhood, 'Now I lay me down to sleep.' That kind of psalm is for children learning to respect and to give thanks. We're here, in this room, to give a helpin' hand, to reach out to the sinner and the lost and the suffering. Don't you think that I or any other pretender to holiness can forgive you. As long as there's a Ruby Jenkins hidden from your view you know that your work is not done, that your prayers are unspoken, that the Lord's plan is unfinished. . . ."

The minister stopped there, seemingly in midsentence. She turned her back and walked away, through an unseen exit, leaving us in the middle of her sermon like survivors of a boat wreck in the center of a vast lake.

It was the shortest sermon I'd ever heard and also the only one to ever touch me.

After a moment of confusion organ music began to play. The sunlight through the abstract designs in the stained-glass windows seemed to brighten. I felt for Theon and his flight from unhappiness; for Jolie who was on the same reckless journey. And I knew that I was, even at that moment, on the same road but that didn't bother me.

"Let's go," Newland whispered in my ear.

The sound of his voice made me gasp and giggle. I stood up like a drunken woman and made my way to the parking lot.

Outside I was reunited with my family, known and unknown. Cornell, who was a few years older than I, glowered, and Delilah (to my surprise) smiled brilliantly. Newland had his arm around the lovely Asian woman's waist, and my mother, Asha Peel, came crying into my arms.

"Sandra, baby," she said.

I held on to her as if for safety in those complex emotional waters.

"Mom," I whispered.

"This is Mi Lin," Newland said as they approached the embrace. "She's my wife."

I smiled and freed a hand to shake.

She grinned with abandon and then laughed.

My mother moved back, holding me only by the wrists now.

"You look so beautiful," she said.

Cornell's glower became a full-out scowl.

Delilah lifted Edison in her arms and came forward.

"You remember your mother, don't you, Edison," she said.

"Uh-huh," he said. "Is it Christmas?"

"No," my stepsister said. "She's finally come home."

There was a look of shocked delight on the boy's face. He stretched out his arms and suddenly I was holding him. His weight was nothing, but my own body felt as dense as stone. Edison squeezed my neck and I had to concentrate not to crush his skinny little body in my arms.

A beautiful and unforgiving black woman came up to Cornell's side.

The world around me seemed to be spinning. I felt like a youngster drunk for the first time. I had moved so quickly from one world into others. This action seemed to resonate with the minister's sermon somehow.

"We're all going to my house for supper,"

my mother said. "You're gonna come, aren't you, Sandra?"

I wanted to say yes. I intended to go. But the overwhelming nature of that day, of the past days, slowed my ability to speak.

"You can bring Theon," she said.

"Theon died, Mom," I said, "but I'll be happy to come to dinner."

"I'm so sorry," Asha said. "Not that you can come but about Theon."

"I'll drive you and the little man," Cornell said to Delilah.

"No, baby," my stepsister said. "We're going to ride with Eddie's mother."

"Yaaaay," my son yelled.

"Uncle Cornell says that you couldn't be my mama no more because you did bad things," Edison said in the car.

He was sitting next to me strapped down by the adult-size safety belt. Delilah was in the back.

"Is that true?" he asked when I didn't respond immediately.

"Eddie," Delilah said.

"No, baby," I said. "What Cornell meant was that the kind of life I was living would have been a bad thing for a child like you. I was protecting you from things that could have made you scared and upset."

"Like what?" he asked.

"You'll find out one day, honey."

"Do you still do things that scare a little kid?"

"Not anymore. No. All that is over as of next Saturday."

"What happen then?"

"I have to go to a funeral and then . . . and then I'm gonna start a whole new life."

"Can I come stay with you?"

I looked up in the rearview mirror.

Delilah had long curly hair that was pulled back and tied with a yellow bow. She had a cherub's face and bright brown skin. One might have called her plain if not for the happiness she exuded. Her eyes were kind and hopeful.

She nodded at me.

"I want you to," I said.

"Then can I?" Edison asked.

"Today is the first day I been back around your grandmother and Delilah and your uncles and aunts," I said. "And so we have to take a few days to figure out what will happen then. I have to find a job somewhere and a new place to live before I can take you with me."

"Is this your car?" my son asked.

"Yes, it is."

"It's nice."

"Thank you."

"Maybe we could live in here."

Delilah laughed and tickled Edison from over the seat.

He laughed too and pretty soon we were all laughing. Before we got to my mother's house Eddie taught me a song about where the little lost donkey goes to get found.

My mother had baked three small butter-basted chickens with white and wild rice stuffing. She quartered the chickens and served them with broccoli spears and canned cranberry sauce. There were three apple-pear pies on the side table for dessert and multicolored pitchers of ice water sweating on the windowsill.

The house I grew up in was small but always seemed large. Even that dining room gave the sense of being a bigger space. It was crowded in there. Along with the people from church there was Winston (who was five), twelve-year-old Margaret, and a baby named James. These three brown children belonged to Yolanda, Cornell's wife. Their father, I was told by Delilah, had been killed in a drive-by shooting.

Yolanda was beautiful in a rough kind of way and looked somewhat familiar.

The sensations of that room cut a deep

and wide swath into my memory. The baby crying and Edison's laughter, Newland's perpetual innocence, and my mother's sense of order and decorum. The smells and sounds, even the air on my skin were reminders of a life I once loved, then hated, and finally forgot for a while in a haze of drugs, sex, and glitter.

"Where'd you and Mi Lin meet?" I asked Newland.

He and his bride were seated across the table from me. On my left side sat my son and on my right was my mother.

"Online," Newland said.

"Really?"

"Lin is from Hong Kong," Newland explained.

Newland was dark and skinny with a round head like my son's. His expression, since he was a baby, was always one of wonder and surprise. He never had trouble with the gangs or the police. No one wanted to hurt Newly, and he was always willing to help you if he could.

"And you were online pen pals?"

"One night I found this Web site about women from other countries lookin' to be American wives," my brother said.

"You should know something about that," Cornell said to me. With that he smiled for the first time I'd seen that day.

"Anyway," Newland continued, "I send 'em a picture of myself and my house and Spider, my dog. I told 'em that I worked for the post office and that I was a sorter.

"Then for a long time I forgot about it — it was almost a year before Mi Lin send me a e-mail."

"I told him," Mi Lin said with a pronounced and yet understandable accent, "that I like what he says more than all the other men, that his pictures were about a real man who lives a real life. His house looks big to me and I like a dog. I work in toy factory and save two thousand dollars. I tell him that if he pay eight thousand I will send him my two for the rest."

"We were all so worried that it was some kinda scam," my mother said. "We told him not to do it."

"But I could tell that she was for real," my brother argued. "You could see it in her pictures and in the way she said what she said. I wrote her back and said that I wasn't rich and that I didn't even have enough to keep her without her gettin' a job, and she wrote back that she liked to work. Boy, you know I hit the credit union the next mornin'. I lied and said I was improvin' my house, but you know I was rentin' then."

"So it all worked out?"

"There was some trouble here and there, but you bettah believe that Mi Lin come here and I married her aftah only three weeks."

"I'm very happy," Mi Lin said.

She grinned at me and I felt a brief surge of amazement. I realized that my little brother, the silly kid asking the same questions over and over in our backyard, had turned into the kind of man whom this woman could love and I could respect — that he had entered life with a steady gaze and even step.

Newland had surpassed me and that made me smile.

"So what about you, Sandra?" Cornell asked.

"What about me?" There was no love lost between me and my older brother, because there was no love to lose.

"What trouble brings you to this house?"

"My husband died."

"And why are you here?"

"Why am I where, Cornell?"

The question threw him. This was a game we had played since we were children. I'd make fun of him and then he'd beat me up.

"Sitting at this table," he said at last.

"Is this your table?" I replied, the playful,

217

willful child in my tone.

"It's our family table."

It came back to me why I had left home. My father was dead and Cornell, for whatever reason, had decided that he was the man of the house. My mother was a helpless wreck and so I received the brunt of my brother's misguided attempts to keep his world from flying apart.

"Cornell," my mother said in a commanding tone I hadn't heard since I was ten.

My brother looked but did not speak.

"This my house," Asha Peel said firmly. "Not yours. You and your family are guests in here. And if you cannot accept and respect your sister on the Lord's day in my house, you don't have to stay."

The silence at that table went way down inside of me. If I had not already decided to give up the adult film world I would have at that moment because of my mother's words.

"I was just sayin' that she don't have a free pass back from the kinda life she been livin', Mama," Cornell said, grasping onto the frayed fabric of a lifetime feeling that he ran our family.

"She has a free pass with me, Cornell. This is my daughter and I will love her no matter what. And if you can't respect her then you show me the same disregard."

"But, Mama . . ."

"That's all, Cornell. You have run rough-shod over Newly and Sandy long enough. I am the elder in this house. Respect me or get out."

Cornell cast a spiteful eye on me. We might as well have been children. He hated me for having a share in our family, and I dared him, for all his superior size and strength, to try to drive me out.

His adopted children sat around Yolanda, their mouths agape, their eyes trying to make out the new patterns of power in the room.

"Why you have to come back, Sandy?" Cornell asked.

My mother got up from her chair and walked out of the room. I followed her.

In her wake I realized how dangerous my brother had been after our father died. It didn't feel like an excuse for the kind of life I'd lived — not even an explanation. It was more like a sudden comprehension of the lay of the land, an aerial view of a terrain I'd always lived in but never really knew.

My mother went to the kitchen door to look out on the overgrown grass of the backyard. She'd already changed out of her maroon Sunday suit into a blue-and-white dress with a complex floral pattern running through it.

"Mama," I said to the back of her graying head.

She turned, I remember, and hugged me fiercely. She was shaking but not actually crying, groaning a low note of remorse.

She leaned away again as she did in the church parking lot, holding me by the wrists. When I looked into her face I saw nothing of me. My mother had a broad, generous look, where I had inherited the long and lean visage of my father.

"I should have told him that a long time ago," my mother said. "I should have stood up for you and Newland when you were still under my roof."

"You were just too hurt when Daddy died like that, Mama. It hurt all of us so bad that none of us knew what to do." I embraced her again.

"But I lost my way," she said. "I lost sight'a my children and they got away from me."

"Not Newland," I said into her lilac-scented hair.

"No," she agreed. "Newly was always my baby. But Corn turnt into a bully and you might as well have been in China."

I cherished those few words between us.

There was no conflict or disagreement, no anger or need for resolution. My mother had been blindsided by the death of the man she loved, and her babies scattered into that darkness like frightened mice running from a sudden, unfamiliar growl.

"You got a cigarette in that li'l bag?" my mother asked.

"You still smoke?"

"So little that you can hardly call it smokin'. It's more like I take a puff now and then."

"Yeah, I got a couple."

At the far end of the backyard, under the clothesline, my mother kept two folding pine chairs. We sat there and I took the nearly empty box of English Ovals from my purse. I brought the handbag with me because of the pistol it contained and the children in the house.

My mother took a drag off the odd-shaped cigarette and sighed.

"That taste good. You still smokin', baby?"

"I haven't had one in days," I said truthfully. "I usually carried them around for Theon. He was always tryin' to quit and then goin' crazy when he found himself without."

"What happened? How'd he die?"

"He got electrocuted. It was an accident."

"I'm so sorry."

"He was a troubled man," I said. "Now those troubles are over."

I breathed in the smoke. It was a warm Sunday and there were no words I needed to say.

"What you gonna do now, Sandy?"

"First I'll bury Theon and then I'll get on with my life."

"Are you still gonna make them movies?"

"No. I'm done with that. It's not that I think it's wrong. I mean, it ain't wrong to work in a coal mine for a dollar a ton . . . it just ain't worth it."

My mother grinned at the phrase my father used to explain his life in the street.

I kissed her on the mouth.

"I missed you, baby," Asha Peel said to me.

"It's been a long time," I agreed.

When we returned to the house Cornell and his family were gone. Delilah had made lemonade for her and Eddie, Mi Lin and Newland. They were sitting in the TV room on the mismatched chairs and sofa there.

Eddie climbed up on my lap and Newland began talking, telling stories as he always did when he had a captive audience.

He regaled us with the minutiae of the

huge post office on Central and Florence.

". . . and, and, and our supervisor, Nia, is what you call a performance poet," he was saying, "and Jack, her boss, collects guns. We got two musicians, three ex-schoolteachers, and just about every race and religion under the sun. It's not like they say — we're not all crazy and antisocial, but you better believe that no two people in that whole buildin' see a glass'a water an' think the same thing."

"You think I could get a job there?" I asked him.

"I think you could do better than that, sis."

"You work there, Newly."

"Yeah," he said. "But only while Mi Lin at school studyin' to be a dental assistant. After she get a job I'ma go to school too."

"And study what?"

"I wanna be an architect. I wanna build houses."

I thought about Rash but didn't mention him. It all seemed too perfect: that I would have met a man who could help my brother — maybe. It was almost a miracle that my mother had stood up and defended me when no one, except my dead father and maybe Theon, ever had.

■ ■ ■ ■

It was hard leaving Edison that evening. He cried and wanted to come with me. Delilah held him up and kissed us both.

Newland walked me to my car.

"What do you think it will do to Delilah if I take Eddie away?" I asked my brother.

"She always told him that she was just holdin' him for you while you got some stuff together. He expects it and so does she."

"It just doesn't feel right."

"Nuthin' felt right since Daddy died, sis. But we got to keep on movin' though, got to."

Theon came to me on the ride from South-Central back to my Pasadena home — not a ghost or apparition, not a hallucination or even a vision. I couldn't see him and I knew he was dead, but still, he was in that car with me giving me the only thing he had in abundance: fear of life and suspicion of potential danger.

"Family seems like a good thing but in the end it's always the family that brings you down," he said, a repetition of a platitude he'd mouthed many times in life.

"My mother loves me," I'd told him once.

"Many men have told you they loved you," he'd said. "They thought they really meant it too."

"What's that got to do with anything?"

"They say it," he said, holding up one finger, "they mean it" — he produced another large digit — "but in the end they will cheat on you, lie to you, and rob you blind. And that's just the momentary kind of love, where there's no blood involved."

"Some man think he love me 'cause he want my ass," I said, disdaining the made-up lover and the remembered husband. "My mother love my soul."

"So did your father," Theon had once said. He'd been drinking and, as always when he was high, he went too far.

"Don't you talk about my father, Theon Pinkney."

"It's the strongest love that makes the greatest treachery," Theon said, instead of backing down like he should have done. I remember being surprised that he even knew how to use the word *treachery*. "The worst thing you can say to somebody is that you will be there no matter what and then fail to show."

I felt the pain in that car the same as I had felt when Theon first said those words.

My daddy was always supposed to be

there. Why was he out that night instead of at home with us? Why did he have to catch that bullet, live that life, make it so that my mother cried for an entire year?

"Love makes you blind to your own survival," Theon went on when I was too hurt to fight him. "And if it doesn't then it's not love at all."

I pulled into my driveway after returning from the bosom of my mother's home. I should have been happy about the love of my son, but instead Theon's words were in my head.

The man grabbed me when I was closing the door to my car. As I was being slammed against the garage door I wondered if Theon was trying to warn me on the drive. Was he trying to tell me that the love of my family might blind me to danger?

"Bitch," Coco Manetti said. "You think you could disrespect me like that?"

He hit me in the midsection and I threw up the butter-basted chicken and canned cranberries.

"Fuck!" he shouted when the vomit hit the left knee of his trousers.

As the backhand slap connected with my face I tried to figure out where my handbag had gone. I was no longer holding it.

"Mothahfuckin' bitch," the white mobster said, mouthing words he'd learned from the part of town I'd just come from.

I took a breath but he hit me in the stomach again and so I lost it. I fell to the concrete and rolled up into a ball. He kicked me and I inhaled while looking around for my purse. He kicked me again and I saw the bag but it was well beyond my reach.

Then Coco Manetti made a mistake. Instead of kicking me more he reached down to lift me up by my arm. I don't know why he did that. Maybe he wasn't getting enough satisfaction from kicking my legs and sides.

I didn't resist the pull.

One thing about my business was that we had to stay in good shape. Our thighs and calves, butts and abdominals had to be strong to keep up those pulsing, derricklike beats hour after hour.

I kicked Coco in the knee and hollered for all I was worth.

Someone shouted, "Who's out there?"

Coco's fist slammed into the side of my head. There was a very bright light in my eyes as a murmuring of fear whispered in the air around my head.

"Over here," a voice called. It was a familiar voice — the one that cried out when I screamed.

Time skipped forward then. I suppose I went unconscious but it didn't feel like that in my head. I thought I had fallen to the ground, heard the various sounds and calls, and almost immediately opened my eyes. But instead of being on the driveway pavement I was lying on a couch in an all-white room with people moving around me. I was in the middle of a conversation with someone but had no idea what we were talking about as I came to awareness within a kind of semiconsciousness.

"Was this the man who attacked you?" Lieutenant Perry Mendelson was asking.

It was hard to concentrate on the kind-hearted cop. My vision wasn't blurred but fragmented, like looking through a broken crystal. I turned in the direction that the policeman was pointing. There I saw two discrete images of Jude Lyon standing with his hands bound behind his back.

"Jude?" I said.

"Hey, Deb."

"Is this the man?" Perry asked again.

"No," I said. "I didn't get a good look at the guy but he was much taller and . . . I know Jude. I'd know if it was him."

"You're sure?"

"Yes."

"We have him in custody, Mrs. Pinkney. He can't hurt you now."

I was reminded of the cops trying to reassure Theon's mother about me.

I forced myself to sit up. There was the smell of vomit rising from my ruined Sunday dress suit.

Four paramedics and three uniformed policemen were moving around the polar bear room. One cop released Jude, who came immediately to my side. I was embarrassed by the way I smelled but grateful to be alive and comparatively unharmed.

"What happened?" Jude asked. His countenance was serious and very masculine. Usually Jude was shy and withdrawn, sometimes petulant, but at that moment he was protective and even a little aggressive.

"Some dude," I said. "He grabbed me from behind and started whalin' on me. I couldn't really see his face."

"Did you hear him saying anything?" Jude asked. "Did you know his voice?"

"No."

"Move aside," Perry Mendelson said to my dead husband's friend.

Jude looked up in anger and defiance. Even in my fractured state of mind I was surprised by his strength and courage in the face of the police.

Finally, after a full five-second stare-down, Jude rose and moved to a sheepskin chair across from the couch.

"Same question, Mrs. Pinkney," Perry said. "Did you recognize anything about your attacker?"

I pretended to think before shaking my head.

"No."

"How about that Richard Ness?"

"He wasn't that big."

"Can you tell us anything at all?"

"What happened?" I asked. "How did you get here?"

"Your neighbor, Miss Alison, called nine-one-one after hearing a scream. When we got here we found Mr. Lyon kneeling over you. He told us that he'd come up and found you on the ground, that he'd already called for help, but we thought that he might have been your attacker."

"I came over to visit, Deb," Jude said, once again in the guise of his mild demeanor. "I was just worried that you might be sad."

"We'd like to take you to the hospital," a paramedic said. "It would be best if a doctor took a look at you, maybe take some X-rays."

"I have my own doctor," I told the sandy-haired, blue-eyed young man.

"I don't know," he said, doubting my decision.

"I'll make sure she gets there," Jude told him.

"I'll need to know where you are," Perry said.

The conversation felt unwieldy, like a juggling act with one too many balls in the air.

"Okay," I said.

"You'll have to sign a release if we don't take you to the hospital," the paramedic said.

"Anything," I told him. "Just stop talking to me."

It took a good forty-five minutes to get the police and ambulance attendants out of my house. Perry asked four times if I wanted Jude to stay.

"Yes," I said for the last time. "He's a family friend."

When they were finally gone I asked Jude to go get me a glass of water while I called Neelo Brown's private line. Neelo asked me if I could get down to his offices and I told him that Jude would take me.

After that things happened in a kind of jumble. I took the pistol out of my purse and told Jude that we'd walk out to his car together. He didn't seem bothered by the gun or the possibility of meeting my attacker again. This brought to mind Theon calling him dangerous.

Jude drove a dark blue Cadillac.

I was sitting next to him drifting in and out of awareness. While driving Jude asked me questions.

"You sure you don't know who attacked you, Deb?" he asked at one point.

"No. No, I don't."

"Because you know you don't have to be afraid."

"No? Why not? I mean, the police wouldn't be able to protect me day and night."

"I'd take care of you."

"You? Come on, Jude. That guy wasn't as big as Richard Ness but he was a foot taller than you."

"Don't let my size fool you," he said. "I can take care of myself."

I fell asleep for a period there. When I woke up we were close to the clinic.

"Did you love Theon?" I remember Jude asking the question when my eyes were closed.

"Sometimes. Did you?"

"Yes," he said. "Yes, I did. Very much."

■ ■ ■ ■

When I opened my eyes again I was in a bed in a private room at Neelo's clinic. The pudgy young doctor was shining a small flashlight into my right eye.

"How you feeling, Aunt Deb?" he asked when I looked directly at him.

"Like somebody dropped a ton of bricks on me and then jumped up and down on them."

"I think you have a concussion but it's mild. You're going to have to rest for a day or two. Do you want me to call anyone?"

"Lana Leer," I said. "Her number's in my red phone. Maybe she could come talk to me later on."

The ocean was a big part of my imagined experience after the beating. I was drifting across the surface a thousand miles from land in a field of seaweed as large as a continent. The floating vegetation kept me buoyant, breathing. The sun was hot and unrelenting. Now and again the air-conditioning came on in the room. The cool breeze made me feel as if I were dunking my head in the water below.

There was a deep concussive sound coming up out of the water. It vibrated through my body, making me laugh and shudder.

The sun wouldn't stop beating down and the waters undulated. I tried to remember why I was there but there was no memory, nothing before the forever ocean and nothing beyond it either.

"Deb? Deb?"

It didn't sound like my name. It wasn't real. It was made up on the spur of the moment and stuck.

"Deb, are you awake?"

I felt flattened and dead, like a fish washed up on the shore then dried out by the sun.

I opened my dry fish eyes and saw Lana sitting on a chair beside the hospital bed. She was wearing a peach-colored dress and a cream fabric hat that flared around the edges like something out of the Roaring Twenties.

"Hi."

"Hey, Deb. How are you, hon?"

"I feel it all the way down between my toes."

"You look pretty good. The swelling went down."

"What day is it?" I asked.

"Tuesday afternoon. You been sleepin' a day and a half."

I tried to rise and failed. My head spun and my intestines felt loose and watery.

"Help me sit up, Lana."

She did this. I managed to get my back against the bars at the head of the bed, feeling that if I leaned to the side I'd fall over and tumble to the floor.

"Neel called me and told me you were here," Lana said. "I called that creepy guy Dardanelle and told him to keep on doin' what he was doin' while you rested."

"What'd he say?"

"He asked who was gonna give the eulogy and I told him you."

I was breathing in through my nose and out through my mouth. My thoughts kept flitting off in tangents about Coco Manetti and my brother — Cornell.

"Deb?"

"Call me Sandy, will ya, Lana? Sandy's my name. She's the woman I want to be." These words invigorated me.

"Okay . . . Sandy."

"You remember the name of that wardrobe and makeup woman?" I asked, then, "The one who used to be in the life but went to work for that movie studio?"

"Bertha. Bertha Renoir."

"Yeah. Could you figure out how to get in touch with her and tell her that I need to talk? You can give her the red phone number."

"You bet."

Lana told me how they replaced my character in Linda Love's film with this girl out of Georgia — named Georgia Peaches — who was four inches shorter and three shades lighter than I. She also had a thick accent even when she was moaning during sex.

Lana left after we had a good laugh and I almost felt strong enough to stand.

I was wanting a book to read when the door opened and a nurse came in. She was short and Korean, stern faced but still pretty in her light blue uniform.

"There's a policeman here to see you, Mrs. Pinkney," she said. "Dr. Brown asked me to ask you if you wanted to see him."

"What's his name?"

"Lieutenant Mendelson."

"Perry," I said to myself, imagining a road in front of me that broke off into so many pathways that it seemed like a fan.

"Mrs. Pinkney?" the nurse said.

"Yes. Send him in."

For a moment the young woman stared at me, as if questioning my ability to make a decision.

"It's okay," I said. "I know him quite well

and I know how to take care of myself."

Time moved in ripples between the young woman's departure and when Perry Mendelson knocked on the door. I thought about calling my mother but Theon's voice interrupted, telling me that family was the quickest route to demolition. I wondered about Rash Vineland and if he'd called over the last two days. And then there was the stone in my passway, Coco Manetti, who seemed to hate me for some reason I couldn't quite grasp.

"Come in," I said to the closed door.

Perry Mendelson was wearing a tan suit and medium blue shirt with a dusky orange tie. There were little clocks on the tie here and there, and there were other shapes, something like yellow commas. It was one of the ugliest ties I'd ever seen and for some reason this enhanced the fondness I felt for the cop.

"How are you?" he asked, approaching the bed.

I nodded and said, "Have a seat."

We were silent a moment there, like short-term lovers who had decided, each on their own, that the relationship would never work.

"You've been having a pretty hard time of it lately, huh?" the policeman said.

"Yeah."

"Have you remembered anything else about the man who attacked you?"

"No. Nothing."

"But you're sure it wasn't Lyon."

"Why do you keep asking that? Jude was a friend of my husband's. He's just a mild little man. I can't imagine him hurting anybody."

"So you really don't know," he said, as if he were having a separate discussion with another me in a different time and place.

"Know what?"

"Your husband's friend is deeply involved with organized crime here in L.A."

"That's ridiculous. What would he be doing with people like Ness?"

"Ness is just a wannabe enforcer," Perry said. "He's nothing compared to Lyon."

"Jude? What could he possibly do that's so bad?"

"He's a person of interest in six murders in Southern California."

Suddenly I was no longer tired or light-headed. A chill ran down the length of my body.

"No."

"He went to college at UCLA studying theater. Him and his friends made their money dealing grass and hash. But they ran into trouble with an outside group that wanted to take over distribution for Westwood. The gang sent out a couple of guys to beat up Lyon's business partner and boyfriend. They went too far and killed him. The two men turned up dead three weeks later, and Jude formed a new gang that drove off the outsiders. Since then he's been the guy people turn to when there's no more talking. No one knows how many people he's killed, but they know the number is higher than what they can put on their charts.

"I've been asked by the squad investigating organized crime in L.A. to get you to help them get something on Lyon."

"You've got to be kidding me," I said. "Even if he wasn't a friend, what you just told me is the fastest way to get killed."

Perry sighed, telling me without words that he'd hoped this would be my answer.

"I'm sorry about taking off my clothes and calling you a perv, Lieutenant."

"No problem, Mrs. Pinkney. Like I said — you've had your share of troubles lately."

"Lately? For the past nineteen years I've compared troubles before getting dressed in the morning."

He smiled and I thought, not for the first time, that we might be friends in a world far different from the one we lived in.

"You really are something else, Mrs. Pinkney."

"Call me Sandy. That's my given name."

"You have to be careful, Sandy," he said. "I'm here unofficially, but other cops will lean on you. They want your friend in prison or dead."

"Why?"

"Because he's a hit man."

"No. Why do you like me? Why are you here?"

We gazed at each other across the small space between the bed and visitor's chair.

Perry tilted his head to the side as he did when he didn't want to tell me that Theon was dead. My question called up an answer that didn't want to come out; it didn't want to but had no choice.

"I spend every day talking," he said. "I talk to cops and criminals, unwilling witnesses, family and friends, bystanders, strangers, and voices on the telephone. And nobody ever says anything that I don't expect. Nobody looks me in the eye and says anything that means something. I don't care if it's a lie or the truth; that doesn't matter. Some people lie to be helpful; that might be the only way to do right. But what I hear is the same old shit over and over.

"But everything you say is on the ground floor. You're right there in front of me like nothing I ever saw."

"I thought you were married, Perry."

"I am. And I will be five years from now. I'm not talking about getting together. Getting together is what everybody expects. If I told my wife how much I like talking to you she'd ask if I wanted a divorce. She wouldn't ask what is it that makes our life feel like it comes out of a box of prefabricated wood and plastic screws. I don't wanna have sex with you. We don't even have to be friends. I just want to do my job and make sure that a wonderful person like you survives this mess."

"Wow." I couldn't think of anything else to say.

"Yeah," he agreed.

I remember that we both smiled and, after a few minutes, Perry stood up. He put a business card on the stand next to the bed and nodded.

"Thank you," he said. Then he left the room.

I took in a deep breath and when I exhaled I felt healed. If I were of my mother's persuasion I would have called myself blessed.

■ ■ ■ ■

Two hours later Neelo, against his better judgment, discharged me. I was wearing clothes that Lana had dropped off from my new purchases. My Jag was in the underground lot — another gift from Lana. I had my blue bag, chrome pistol, and red phone. Life was flowing on and I wouldn't have been able to change course even if I wanted to.

I connected the phone to the speaker system of my car and listened to the messages.

"Hi," Rash Vineland said. "I'm crazy for you. I will do, or . . . I won't do anything to be with you. Call me and tell me when I can see you again."

I would surely call him. I worried, though, that his life might be ripped up over the feelings he harbored.

"We didn't get to finish our dance," Coco Manetti said. "I'm looking for you. So either you hide or you give me what I want."

The one thing I was sure of, the thing Perry told me with a sigh, was that the police would not save me from men like Manetti. I would have to dig myself out of that hole alone — either that or be buried in it.

"Hello?" a mild male voice answered on the second ring.

"Jude?"

"Hey, Deb," he said. "How are you?"

"Can I meet with you?"

"Sure. When?"

"Now."

"Okay. I'm at the Bread and Chocolate Theater on Robertson and Olympic."

"I know the place."

It was a small, eighty-seat theater behind an Oriental rug store on Robertson. There was no marquee, just a glass-encased space the size of a movie poster with a list of the performances and events going on at the playhouse. The double doors were ajar and I walked in without anyone challenging me.

A red-haired young woman was sitting in a folding metal chair just inside the theater doors. She was reading a script and chewing gum.

"Excuse me," I said.

"Uh-huh?"

"I'm looking for Jude Lyon."

"Judy? Yeah, he's in the house. You work for him?"

"Yes. He asked me to drop by."

"Go on in," she said, and before I could thank her she was back in her manuscript.

The whole room, stage and seating, was brightly lit. There were carpenters and painters banging, sawing, and painting on the set. Jude was standing to the side of the slightly elevated stage, looking at the work with a serious eye. When I walked in he seemed to sense my presence and turned to look at me.

He smiled.

I gave him a little wave and he jogged over.

We kissed cheeks. He took me by the wrists and examined my face.

"You don't look much the worse for wear," he said.

"Neelo's a good doctor."

"What can I do for you, Deb?"

"Can we get a cup of coffee?"

"Sure," he said, and then he turned toward the stage and piped, "Hey, boys, me and the girl are going to powder our noses. See you in twenty."

As we walked from the theater I wondered at the many faces of Jude Lyon.

Whenever I saw him with Theon or as an escort he was a timid, shy man — not masculine, not flaming. It made me smile to think that even the bedrock of my beliefs was soft and yielding.

In the coffee shop Jude ordered us lattes

and chocolate croissants. We brought these to a little round table set in the window, removed from any other seats and on display to the world.

We sat there for a while in silence, our food and drink forgotten. There was no room for small talk between us right then.

"So, did they figure out who attacked you?" he asked at last.

I shook my head and said, "The police came to my hospital room and told me that they thought you were some kind of criminal and that they wanted me to try to help them trip you up. I told them no, but I wanted you to know what they were saying."

I knew from Jude's blank expression that the things Perry said were true. His eyes turned feline, filled with the kind of trouble no one ever saw coming.

"I don't need you to talk to me about it," I added. "I just wanted to say that they're looking at me now and you should be careful calling me or talking in my house or car or whatever. Not that you've ever said anything. Theon didn't either."

While I spoke, and after, Jude scrutinized me. His brown eyes, under slightly creased brows, could have been humming — he was that intent.

"Are you frightened?" he asked.

"No."

"Why did you come to me?"

"You've been really good to me. And anyway, you were always nice to Theon. I don't need to help the cops take down my friends."

He sat back and picked up his paper coffee cup. Suddenly he was a mild-mannered little man again.

"Why do you act so different in different places?" I asked then.

"What do you mean?"

"I never knew anybody to call you Judy, for instance."

Jude smiled.

"I love the theater," he said. "The people there are so wrapped up in stories, and how they look in those stories, that they don't pay so much attention to you. It's like being in a thick forest where sound doesn't travel far and the sun is weak. It's like you're hidden so deep that you don't even know where you are."

I nodded uncertainly and bit into my fancy French pastry.

"Who beat you, Deb?"

I decided to stay Deb with Jude. I also, somewhat contradictorily, determined not to lie to him.

"I'd really rather not say."

He nodded.

"I never trusted you," he said. "I always thought that you were using Theon somehow. I guess it was because I was so enchanted with him. He was quite a guy. Crazy and lost but he could be a good friend. He never told you about what I did?"

"Never."

"And that doesn't bother you?"

"Why would it? I knew you guys were friends. Even if it was more than that, we never had an exclusive relationship — sexually. How could we? I have lots of friends who tell me secrets that I'm not supposed to tell. If it didn't have to do with Theon directly, he didn't expect to know them, and neither did I."

Again Jude took a sip of his coffee. He watched me as an infant might study some new person who had come into his line of sight.

"Are you wired?" he asked.

"No."

He took a bite of bread and wondered some more.

"I need to know who beat you, Deb. I owe Theon at least that much."

Something in his tone reassured me. I had kept quiet about the gangster because I didn't think that anyone could help me with him. Now I wasn't so sure.

"Coco Manetti."

"From Manhattan Beach?"

"I don't know where he's from. Theon owed Richard Ness money, but when he came to collect I pulled a gun on him. I guess he got scared, 'cause he sold the debt to Manetti."

"How much you owe him?"

I told him.

"Theo invested money with me," Jude said, "in one of my businesses. That's what I do. I take investments, buy product, and distribute. A certain percentage goes back to my investors. I was thinking, because Theon died, that the profit would stay with me, but I guess the money he gave me was yours, huh?"

"I was the only one making a salary."

"I can have what you owe Manetti in an hour. You could call him and make a six-o'clock meeting at a place I know — the Black Forest Restaurant."

"Uh . . . okay."

I didn't tell Jude that I knew what the cops suspected him of. I didn't expect to get the money I owed Manetti. I really didn't know what I was doing. But I couldn't refuse the cash. Getting Manetti off my back would ease my life greatly.

Using the number he called me from, I called Manetti from the coffee shop.

"Yeah?" he answered.

"It's Theon's wife," I said.

"You ready to do what I asked?"

"Meet me at six at the Black Forest Restaurant on Melrose."

"This better not be some trick," he said.

After the call I drove Jude to a house in the Bel-Air area. He went in and came out with a small satchel.

"This is a hundred and twenty-seven thousand," he said, "in two packages. The one with the blue X on it is seventy-two thousand. The other one contains the rest. Now you can drop me off at the playhouse, go meet Coco, and settle the debt."

"It doesn't feel that easy."

"It will be," Jude said with a conviction I found it hard to deny.

Jude's certainty lost its strength when I was sitting at the mostly empty restaurant. It was an open room with a broad west-facing window. Light poured in over the potted bamboo plants placed here and there to break up the seating. I was sipping a merlot with the black leather satchel on my lap.

After dropping Jude off at Bread and

Chocolate I stopped in a garage and took the plastic-wrapped package without the blue X and put it in the trunk. For a full fifteen minutes I considered picking up Edison and going to Texas or North Carolina to start a new life. But I couldn't put my son in that kind of jeopardy and I wouldn't leave without him.

That was an important moment for me. I realized if I were to survive, I needed to be with my boy.

I had no idea who his father was. Because of his dark coloring I supposed that he was a black man. There were about thirty possibilities. For some reason my birth-control regimen had been thrown off and somebody's sperm made it through the war zone of my womb.

Theon was great while I was pregnant. He took on some directing jobs and spent the rest of his time at home. He wanted to keep Edison, but even if Cornell hadn't threatened to call child services, I knew that our lifestyle would not be good for a kid.

"Ms. Dare," a man said. It was Coco. He was wearing a gray suit that gave the impression that it was made of metal. He smiled and sat down across from me, an evil Tin Man from an alternate Oz.

I tried to speak but failed. I realized that

coming there was a mistake. The leer on Manetti's face told me that he now saw me as submissive. I had to suppress the urge to shoot him then and there.

"You ready to make some movies?"

"I got you your money," I said, hefting the little satchel and placing it on the table.

"Seventy-two thousand?" he said as he shifted in his chair.

"Yes."

"What about the interest?"

"What interest?"

"Two thousand dollars a day late fees. That's eight thousand more."

"Can I bring you something to drink?" a waiter asked Manetti. He seemed to appear out of nowhere.

"Go away," Coco said.

"Can I get you another glass of wine?" the waiter then asked me.

"Didn't I tell you to go away?" Coco asked.

"I wasn't speaking to you, sir," the server said quite pleasantly. "I was speaking to the lady."

"You better get the fuck away from here."

The waiter might have been a fool but I appreciated him. He waited to see if I had anything to add and, when I didn't, he walked off at a leisurely pace.

"One way or another you're going to work for me," Coco said.

"No."

"You need to make a film for a friend of mine," he said, "to pay your vig. We got it all set up. The shoot starts next Monday."

"I can't do that, Mr. Manetti."

"No? The next time I beat on you there won't be anyone around to stop me."

"Hello, Coco," someone said.

He was standing right next to us but neither of us had any inkling of his approach. It was Jude in a very nice, dark Armani suit. He smiled as the waiter from before pulled a chair up to the table.

Coco was so surprised that he didn't respond.

"Deb," Jude said in greeting.

"Hey, Jude." I liked saying that.

"What are you doing here?" Coco asked, if not with deference at least with respect.

"This is my restaurant. I own the place."

"We're doing some business," Coco said, trying to regain control at the table.

"I didn't know that you had anything to do with Deb. What's in the bag?"

"Nuthin'."

"I only ask," Jude said, "because I gave a bag just like that to Deb only an hour ago.

252

We're very good friends, you know. Very close."

Coco gave me an evil stare.

"I don't appreciate people fucking with my friends," Jude added. "I don't like it when they try to extort them either."

"I bought her debt."

"You bought Theon Pinkney's debt. Deb never borrowed a cent, did she?"

"Listen, man —"

"I asked you a question in my house," Jude said, cutting the gangster off.

Again Coco was silent.

"You know me, Coco," Jude said in a soothing tone. "I'm a fair guy. I don't push people around. I mind my own business. But Theon was my friend and Deb here is too. You have no reason to make her pay for an act of God; neither does Dick Ness."

"So what you sayin', Jude?"

"Mr. Lyon."

"What do you want?"

"Give Deb her money back and tell Dick from me that he should repay you. If he doesn't like that he knows where to find me. If he needs a friend in some of his work he can call me then too. How's that?"

"I've wasted time on this."

"Time lived is an eternal blessing," Jude Lyon quoted from somewhere.

Coco's nostrils flared. He pushed the leather bag six inches across the table in my direction. Then he stood up, refusing to look at me. I knew by this avoidance that I was safe.

As Coco walked out of the restaurant I said, "Thanks, Jude. Thanks a lot."

"Theon knew that he could pay off Ness but he died before we saw each other. And Dick and Coco know there's no insurance in the loan-sharking business. Call me if you need anything else."

Jude left soon after Coco. I stayed because I didn't trust my legs to carry me or my hands to steer a three-ton automobile.

I ordered pounded pork chops with brussels sprouts and new potatoes and waited for the food to come. My mother was crying somewhere in a room far away and long ago. She was crying, night after night, because my father was out with his thug friends getting into trouble, breaking the law.

When he'd come home my mother stayed in the bedroom while Aldo poured himself a drink in the dining room.

On one such evening, when I was ten, I climbed out of bed and went to see my father while his wife dried her tears and waited.

"Hey, baby girl," he said when I walked in. He was drinking scotch and smoking a filterless cigarette.

"Daddy?"

He held out his arms and I ran to sit in his lap.

"Yeah, babe?"

"How come you stay out late with them men an' make Mama cry?"

It was a dangerous question. Aldo Peel had a bad temper and when he was mad anything could happen. I knew I was risking something terrible, but still I needed to know why my mother had to suffer.

Instead of shouting and throwing me to the floor my father laughed. He kissed my cheek and hugged me tightly.

"Does that make you mad?" he asked.

"It makes me feel bad for Mama. I don't like it for her to be so sad."

"You don't like it and I don't neither," he said. "You think I wanna be out in the street with them fools? You think I wouldn't rather be in the house with my wife and children?"

"Then how come you don't stay home?"

"Because I will not be a slave, dear heart." He took a deep drag off his cigarette.

"I don't understand, Daddy."

"This country is run by big men," he said. "There ain't too many of 'em. Most the men in this land is little like me and all the other men an' women on this block, in this neighborhood. The big men put all the little people in cages so small that a little man or woman got to ask the big man to open the door just to turn around."

"Like a jail?" I asked.

Aldo Peel nodded vigorously. "Except the do' ain't locked. The little man could walk outta there anytime he wanted."

"Then why don't he?"

My father brought his face very close to mine. I remember clearly the sour scent of cigarettes and whiskey.

"Because the only way the little people could eat is to stay in that cage like the do' really was locked. Even if they just open the do' to turn around without askin' they don't eat that week.

"That's why I go out at night. That's why I run with bad men and do things they say is wrong — because I will not live in the big man's cage. I will not be his punk."

I wanted to hold my father right then. I wanted to shield him from the big men and their power.

"Aldo," my mother said from the doorway behind me.

My father kissed me on the lips and hugged me to his chest. There were tears in his eyes when he put me down.

My mother told me to go to bed and then took my father by his waist and walked him to their bedroom.

I didn't go to bed but instead stayed at the dining room table, sitting in the chair where my father sat. I understood something that I could not have explained, something that I would have forgotten if I had gone to bed like my mother said. I stayed up all night, until the birds were singing and the sun reached around the far corner of the earth, because I needed to hold on to the sad truth my father had transmitted to me.

I sat in the darkness, and then in light, imagining the world as long hallways of small cells holding all of my friends and their parents and all of their friends. Giant men and women with bullwhips patrolled the hallways, snapping at hands and feet that stuck out from the cells. People were crying and moaning like my mother. Electric light filtered down through the bars and I knew that there was no sunlight or moonlight anywhere in that world.

"Excuse me," a woman said.

257

I looked up from my half-eaten meal to see a young white woman with bleached hair and a silver stud on the left side of her nose.

"Yes?"

"We're getting ready to close up."

"Oh."

I sat in the driver's seat of my car for more than an hour, afraid to turn the ignition. The scenario of the night my father kissed me kept going through my mind. I understood now, twenty years later, that X-rated moviemaking had become my cage. When Coco said that I had to work for him I realized that either I would shoot myself or him at that table. I would not, like my father would not, go back into that cold cell.

This conviction finally overcame my fears and I drove home at a normal speed, managing to keep my wheels within the lines but wanting to crash into every car and pedestrian I passed.

Anna Karin's office was on Wilshire not far from La Cienega. It was on the third floor of a boxy brown office building. I was at her gray door by five fifty the next morning, Wednesday. I knocked and, after a brief wait, she pulled the door open and smiled.

She was wearing a coral-colored dress with a string of light green stone beads around her neck.

The office was as I remembered: rented furniture that was designed for function and not beauty. I'd shot many a sex scene in offices like this one, anonymous rooms that some secretary leased on the sly.

"I like your outfit," Anna said of the tan-and-blue dress I wore.

"Thanks."

I made it to the brown leather chair that was there for her patients. She sat on a maple chair that had a checkered cushion as its seat. The window behind her looked out on Wilshire and there were paintings of forest scenes on three walls.

"You said that your first session was at eight, didn't you?" I asked.

"Yes."

"Then why did you want me here at six?"

"Because I have the feeling we might go over and I didn't want to rush you or have my next patient wait."

"How are we going to do this?" I asked.

"Nothing has changed," she said, smiling. "We'll talk and try to see where you are."

"I haven't shaved my cunt or fucked anybody in over a week."

"Hiatus?"

259

"I quit."

"What are you going to do now?"

"I have absolutely no idea."

I could see by Anna's face that she wanted to smile; maybe there was even a laugh dammed up behind her faltering professionalism.

"I think we should start from the beginning," she suggested.

I went at the story like a novice craftsman practicing laying brick. I'd gone over it a hundred times in my head and told parts of the tale to this one and that. When I'd come to the end I'd knock it over, a child with her blocks, and then build again — each time constructing a slightly different explanation.

The events were familiar in my mouth. The only difference with Anna Karin is that I told her everything.

I included the gun and my intentions to kill or die, the fact that I knew Jolie, and even what happened between Coco and Jude.

"Did you ever want to shoot Cornell?" she asked at one point.

"No . . . never."

"Are you still considering suicide?" she asked at another juncture.

"Only when I think that I might have to

260

go back to making films."

I'd been regaling her for well over an hour when she said, "Tell me more about this orgasm you had on the set."

"It was nothing special. . . . I mean it didn't have to do with Theon or Jolie — I didn't even know that they were dead yet. It's just that . . . I don't know. . . ."

"Do you often have orgasms on the set?"

"I'm too busy pretending to have any real feeling."

"Then why did you have one that day?"

The question was like the sounding of a huge Buddhist gong. It vibrated in the air around me. Instead of ideas the experience of that room came back to me. I could hear Carmen Alia's camera clicking and buzzing and the footsteps of the cameramen as they shifted with the gyrations Myron was putting me through. I heard Linda Love's voice but not the words, and most of all, I felt the hot lights on my skin. It was music and it was dance and I was a dead woman being flung about in the pretense of celebration and abandon, and somewhere in the rising and falling, the lifting and heartlessness . . . I came alive.

"It just all came together," I said. "The sounds and light, the pain inside me. It just all came together and I was coming harder

261

than I ever had — ever."

"Did you enjoy it?"

"No, not at all. As a matter of fact I wanted to get away from it. It was like I passed out on purpose just to stop feeling."

For a while there we were both quiet. I appreciated the silence and wondered why I had that sexual awakening as Theon was dying. What sense did it make? It was as if, in some cockeyed way, we traded places.

"What will you do?" Anna Karin asked me.

"I like reading books."

"What will you do for work?"

"That'll come," I said. "I have to finish quitting before I can start working again."

Anna smiled then.

"Can I go now?" I asked.

"See you tomorrow morning?"

"You bet."

At nine o'clock I was at a park bench just outside the fenced-in La Brea Tar Pits, looking at the plaster statue of a great woolly mammoth stuck and being pulled down into the muck.

The red phone in the blue bag rang.

"Hello."

"Hey, Aunt Deb," Dr. Neelo Brown said,

262

"I have someone here who wants to talk to you."

The phone made some transfer noises and then a masculine voice said, "Hello?"

"Yes?" I said. "Who's this?"

"Willie Norman, Mrs. Pinkney."

"How are you feeling?"

"I just wanted to thank you, ma'am, for putting me together with Dr. Brown and making it so that I could get my spells under control."

"Neelo's been treating you?"

"Uh-huh. Yeah. I never went to no doctor before 'cause I didn't think they could do anything, but Dr. Brown gave me these pills and this light I could look at and now I'm almost perfect. So I just wanted to tell you thanks from me and, and, and Tai too. And I wanted to tell you that you don't have to worry about my car. I can fix that myself."

"Thank you, Willie. Thanks a lot."

"And I wanted to say that I'm sorry about your husband. I'm sorry he died."

Anna Karin asked me if I wanted to kill myself and I told her that the idea entered my mind only when I thought about making films again. But I realized later that that wasn't the case, I wrote in my pilfered journal: *The truth is I'm thinking about it all*

263

the time. It's like a door open at the side of the house and this cool breeze is blowing in over the back of my neck. The breeze is Death whispering and that door is open for me to go through anytime I want. And I want to go through. I want the confusion to stop — no, not only confusion but pain too.

In Anna's office I realized that fucking Myron Palmer somehow jump-started me back to life like a woman finding herself suddenly awake after years and years in a coma. It hurts to feel all these things and to know that all I have to do is shut them off again and the pain will stop.

Just breathing hurts me. Feeling love for my son hurts me. The idea of the sun shining cuts at me with red-hot blades. . . .

The phone was ringing again.

"Hello," I whispered.

"Deb? It's Bertha, Bertha Renoir."

"Hey, Bertha," I said, feeling real pleasure at hearing her voice. "It's been so long, girl."

"Uh-huh, it sure has. Lana called and told me about Theon. That's a shame. I'm so sorry for your loss."

"Thank you. I guess he went out the way he would have wanted, though."

"At least he didn't take you with him."

I was remembering how blunt and straightforward Bertha was. That was a real help in movie makeup; subtlety did not show up on digital shots.

"I'd love to get together with you and talk, B, if you have the time."

"That's what Lana said. I'm up north of Malibu on a surfing movie shoot. You could come up anytime today."

She gave me the directions and I scribbled them down below my notes about death.

I was on my way to Malibu when the red phone rang again.

"Hello?" I said into the multidirectional car microphone.

"Hey . . . It's me."

"Hey, Rash. I'm sorry I haven't called you, hon. You wouldn't believe the things been going on."

"Oh, um, well, yeah . . . I know that you're a very busy woman. I guess I just wanted to know . . ."

"It's okay, honey. I wanted to call but I really couldn't. This funeral thing has been a bitch, and I had to deal with that guy Coco."

"Did you work it out?"

"Will you come to the funeral? It's gonna be Saturday at two forty-five at Day's Rest Cemetery."

"I didn't know your husband."

265

"You'll be there for me."

After a long silence he said, "Okay. All right. I'll be there."

"There's another call," I said, looking at the monitor above the rearview mirror. "I'll talk to you later.

"Hello?" I said, after disconnecting Rash by answering the next call.

"Hi, Sandy," Delilah Peel, my stepsister, said.

"Hey, Deihl. How you doin'?"

"You wanna come by tonight, hon? I think Edison expects to see you."

The sensual feeling of suicide flitted through my mind and body. I wondered why.

"How you feelin' 'bout all this, Deihl?"

"He's your son."

"But you raised him. You been there for all his first days and bruised knees. When he wakes up scared in the middle'a the night you the one, the one he calls to."

"He asks God to bless you in his prayers every night."

"But you the one sits there when he gets down on his knees."

"A boy needs his mama, Sand; you know I will not stand in the way'a that."

"I'll come by tonight. I'll be there."

The rest of the ride I felt a thrumming in

my body. The idea of ending my life increased with the passing minutes. I had thought I'd left that feeling in the Malibu mountains, but as I returned to that enclave of wealth and beauty the yearning for release returned.

The movie, *Surf's Inn,* was being shot on the beach a mile or so north of Sunset. Seeing the small production sign, and the row of trailers, I pulled in.

"I'm sorry, miss," a young white man with reddened skin and bulging biceps told me. "This is a closed set."

"My name's Deb," I said, "and I'm here to see Bertha Renoir."

The young man frowned. There must have been a few of the younger Hollywood lions on the set. That meant there were all kinds of fans and paparazzi trying to get in.

"Deb who?"

"Dare."

There was a moment of stunned realization in the young man's eyes. He had seen me in action before: my shaved pussy and swollen clit. He'd stared at my perfect-looking breasts and listened to thousands of my sighs feigning pleasure. He looked at my short hair and almost asked a question but then got on his walkie-talkie. He moved away from my car but I could see by his shoulder movements that he was arguing with someone.

Finally he turned back to me and said, "Go to the pink trailer on the right-hand side."

"I know which one it is."

Bertha's trademark was the pink trailer that looked like it just pulled out of a fifties campsite somewhere in America's heartland. Inside that mobile space she had clothes and wigs, every shade of makeup imaginable, and accessories from feather boas to leather bow ties.

"Hey, Deb." Bertha was chubby and beautiful, probably in her fifties but she looked ten years younger. Her skin was delicate and pale.

"B," I said.

"Come on in and sit down."

On her makeup chair sat a barely legal white girl wearing only a bikini thong bottom. While we talked Bertha was covering the girl's body with various forms of creams and powders.

"I'm so sorry to hear about Theon," Bertha said.

"Yeah. Thanks, hon."

"It's a hard trade," Bertha said. "That's

why I got out of it. Too many people died and too few mattered.

"Jo-Jo at the front gate was tryin' to tell me that it wasn't really you. He thought that because you didn't have long white hair and a tattoo that it couldn't be. Nice job on the makeup over the stain.

"Okay, Juanita," she said, slapping the bikini actress's ass. "You can go out and frolic with your friends."

Juanita giggled and got up. She was short and thin, except for her butt.

"Miss Dare," she said from the doorway. "It . . . it's a real honor meeting you."

She tittered again and skipped out into the sunshine.

Bertha put a sign on her door and closed it.

"I worked past my break waitin' for you to come, hon," she said. "So we have some time."

She sat me in her client's chair and placed her stool across from me. She didn't offer me anything to drink, not because she was rude but because Bertha lived a life where you asked for what you needed or else you went without.

"I see you're married," I said, referring to the rose gold band on the wedding finger.

"His name is Tommy Blueblood."

"You're kidding."

"Uh-uh, real name. I'm Bertha Blueblood now."

"What does he do?"

"He makes jewelry from semiprecious stones that he polishes himself. It's really very cool and he's a great guy."

"I'm happy for you," I said, trying to find the feeling those words expressed.

"How you holdin' up?" the makeup artist asked.

"I don't know," I said truthfully. "I mean, I don't feel bad or anything. I cried once and everything's different now. I quit the business. And even though everything seems fine I think about killing myself when there's nothing else going on."

"Are you taking something for that?"

I smiled to think that there might be an antisuicide pill in the world.

"I'm seein' a shrink."

"That's good," the chubby woman said with a nod. "You know there's no reason for somebody to take their life away. Uh-uh."

"You know, B, I came here to have you do something for the funeral."

"I already gave that Dardanelle my credit card, baby. I gave him a hundred and fifty dollars."

"Are you coming?"

"Oh yeah. Me and Tommy will be there. He's never met my old crowd and says he wants to."

"Do you think you can come early and bring me some stuff?"

"What do you need?"

Bertha walked me out of the pink trailer and went with me toward my car.

"Bertha," a young man called.

He was wearing a yellow Hawaiian shirt and khaki cutoffs. A thirtysomething white man, he was handsome in a rugged sort of way. He looked familiar.

"Hey, Johnny," Bertha said in a tone that let me know that he was important. "This is my friend — Deb."

"Hi," he said, hitting me with a killer smile. I could feel the strength in his hands but his grip was gentle.

"This is Johnny Preston," Bertha said even as I recognized him.

"Oh. I think you were doing business with my husband."

"Who's he?" the affable star asked.

"Theon Pinkney."

"Yes, indeed. He put up the money for a heist script I'm producing. It's called *Inside Out*. We're hoping to shoot it next spring.

You can tell Theon that."

"He died," I said.

"Oh." The actor put on an appropriate frown. "I'm sorry, Mrs. Pinkney. So sorry."

"Thanks," I said. "So . . . you think you're gonna make the film?"

"You never know," he said, producing that well-rehearsed smile again. "I want to. I get to play a homicidal maniac. Maybe if they like it I won't have to do any more surf films."

I smiled and nodded.

"It'd be great to get the script money back," I said. "Theon died kinda broke."

"You'll know when I do. His accountants, uh . . ."

"Chas and Darla?"

"Yeah. They've been on top of my manager."

"Hey, Johnny," a young woman called from down toward the beach.

"That's my scene," he said to me.

We shook hands and he sprinted away toward the cameras.

"That's my son's college fund," I said to Bertha.

"Theon was a good guy," she said, "but nobody could ever blame him for being too smart."

■ ■ ■ ■

Suicide sat next to me on the ride back from the beach. He was the same olive-skinned gentleman who was in the periphery when I had my orgasm. He was sleek and cool in a dusky gray sharkskin suit, in every way someone you'd want to know and whom you were afraid of at the same time. His smile was understanding, even friendly. He was armed but wouldn't hurt you unless you crossed him.

My fingertips were numb, my lips too.

Suicide smiled easily. He wasn't Death but merely an intermediary, like that door left ajar at the side of the house.

I knew he wasn't really there next to me but I also knew that he was real. He'd been my bodyguard since the day my father died. He was my exit strategy, my best friend and guardian angel.

Mr. Suicide was as tangible as the blood in my veins, as the midnight special in my purse. He was why no one could hurt me or bully me or make me into something I didn't want to be.

Suicide was a messenger who kept in constant contact with Aldo, my father.

"What do you want from me?" I dared to

ask him as we crossed Sepulveda headed east on Pico.

He didn't answer but his smile was resplendent.

"I need you to tell me," I said, even though I was mostly sure that he wasn't there.

Stopping at the next red light I turned my head to regard him.

His race was indiscernible, nonexistent among the varieties of men. He was a god, perfection, as real as the sky and as distant.

A sexual friction was rising in my lower abdomen. It was slick and bloody, vibrating at an incredible, feathery rate. It was the feeling I had for Theon when I was living at his place but we had not yet become lovers.

His interim girlfriend had been Venus Moxie, a frequent costar in his various films. They would do lines of coke and fuck in the living room where I watched TV. Theon would have his eyes on me while Venus rode his incessant erection.

I loved the attention. It made me feel that he belonged to me even if he was with her.

A horn honked loudly and I realized that I'd drifted out of my lane.

I pulled to the curb on Motor and took in deep breaths. Suicide was semitransparent there next to me. Theon and Venus were memories threatening to become real in the backseat. My fingers were numb, my wrists were burning, and I felt like I did just before stupid Myron Palmer made me come.

Everything was sex: the soles of my feet, the crazy bone in my left elbow, the smell of my sweat and perfume. I wanted to get down on my knees and have some nameless, tattooed biker fuck me with his bent dick. I wanted Suicide to take me without having to give him a thing.

Was that possible?

I pulled up in front of the lime-green bungalow on Darton Street just as the sun kissed the horizon. The sky had turned an iridescent orange and black from the sunset, cloud cover, and air pollution. On the way I had to pull my car to the curb eight times to avoid losing control.

I wanted to die but every time I imagined it a sexual tension ignited in me and the wish for death turned into a need for sex. This agony was exquisite and depleting. It took a quarter of an hour to climb out of the car and go to the door of the small house.

"Mama!" Edison yelled as he flung the door open.

275

I dropped to my knees and he rushed into my arms. I held on to him as if he were a single jutting stone in the middle of the ocean and I was a drowning woman fresh from a shipwreck.

"How are you, baby?" I asked.

He squeezed me for an answer.

"Did you save your mama something to eat?"

"Come on," he said.

He took me by the hand and dragged me into the manicured living room. Delilah wore a cranberry pantsuit, standing there like a saleswoman for a well-maintained furniture showroom. The sofa and its companion stuffed chair were blue and plush. The floor was dark oak, as was the coffee table.

There was a gray cardboard box in the corner, overflowing with Edison's toys. I imagined him straightening up his little boy's mess for me while I was out in my car struggling to survive long enough to see him.

Delilah smiled. She was shorter than I, with big eyes and freckles across her copper-and-gold face. She was a few pounds over her perfect weight and lovely to me.

"Hi," she said with a smile that added intention to the greeting.

276

"Hey."

"Come on, Mama," Edison said. "We got pizza in the kitchen."

It was hard for me to fit into that evening with my son and stepsister. Edison showed me his room and his toys, his books and secret treasures. I paid attention like a forensic accountant gauging the worth of my little boy's life.

Delilah loved him and cared for him in ways that I might never be able to. He could read at least a dozen words and he could count. He said *please* and *thank you* without reminder, and he was healthy and unafraid.

In other words — he didn't need me. Delilah had brought him up into childhood with no scars or frowns on his face.

He loved me but he needed what my father's adopted daughter had to offer. And she loved him; I could see that love in each gesture and in every corner of her home.

We watched a cartoon movie about a little beaver named Barney who had been driven out of the forest by a fire and who had to make a life for himself in the city. There he met cats and dogs, humans and other displaced forest denizens, struggled to survive, and finally found a natural paradise where the waters were clear and there was need for a dam.

By the end Edison and Delilah were both sound asleep. My hands felt huge, like baseball mitts. My head ached and my legs were numb but ambulatory.

I put Edison to bed and then woke up Deihl.

She gave me a sleepy smile and kissed me.

"You wanna stay the night?" she asked.

"I think I better. I really don't feel like drivin'."

She got me sheets and a blanket and fitted them to the cushions of the blue sofa.

"Me and Eddie are off early in the morning," she said.

"Not early as me."

There are states other than wakefulness and sleep. There is, for instance, the kind of unrest when you are so close to consciousness that you are not really out. You're still there in the world — just separated by a thin barrier of black tissue.

I lay there on the couch thinking about dreams and dreaming of ideas. Theon was there with me trying to distract my train of thought. He was grumbling that I wasn't paying attention. My hands and feet were swollen and I said, "Give me a break, man.

I'm trying to let you go."

There were debt collectors sitting across from the sofa, each with a briefcase full of bills that they wanted me to pay; each hiding an erection in his pants, as interest — these two words, *erection* and *interest,* hung in the air unrealized and definite.

I was lying there in the darkness but I could see everything quite clearly. I was attempting to trace my steps backward from the parking lot just south of Hollywood Boulevard where I gave blow jobs for fifteen dollars and was just about to meet Theon. I was trying to back into the life with my mother and brothers, my stepsister and long-ago friends Maxine, Oura, Maryanne, and Juan.

I was walking backward, away from the smelly john's car, down La Cienega Boulevard, past the vice squad police cars headed up toward the avenue. I was going backward in time but everything else was going forward. It was very awkward, moving in reverse through life, but I kept it up because I couldn't live on the path I'd already traveled. I got all the way back to my mother's house, my childhood home.

I walked backward through the front door. In the entranceway Cornell had a baseball in his hand but decided not to throw it at me. He looked confused and I smiled at him, moving past him in time and space, avoiding his tortures.

I made it all the way to the living room. There I stopped and found myself once again on the sleeping sofa in Delilah's house almost twenty years later. The front door banged open and my father staggered in, bleeding from the bullet wound in his chest. The debt collectors scattered. Theon stopped complaining.

"Daddy!" I screamed, and he fell on me, bleeding and choking on the blood.

I came awake in the dark room no longer able to see through the gloom. I was panting, a prayer fragment in my mind. ". . . and protect Mama and Daddy from harm."

My red phone showed me that it was four twenty-six in the morning. I stood up, feeling dizzy and weak. I sat down and thirty minutes passed in what felt like an instant. I stood up again and dressed.

It was six-oh-one when I got to Anna Karin's gray door that morning. I couldn't remember the last time I'd been late for an appointment.

Anna smiled when she opened the door and moved her body in such a way as to invite me in.

I went to the brown leather seat as she sat in the straight-backed maple chair.

"I've been thinking of suicide every other minute since I left yesterday morning," I said.

"Really? Are you seriously considering it?"

"No," I lied, "not really. It's just in my mind after we talked about it. Why do you think that is?"

"What do you think?"

"I think that the power over death and life is the greatest strength that any person can have. It trumps sex and wealth. If I'm willing to die no one can master me."

"Do you feel that people are trying to control you?"

"Dead people," I agreed. "Theon and my father mainly. They have a hold on my heart. I can't seem to get away from them no matter what I do."

"Maybe you shouldn't try to pull away," Anna said. "Maybe you should face their deaths and come to terms with the reality."

"The reality is that I'm more a part of them than I am a part of anything in this world. I went to see my son, Edison, last night. He was so happy. He wants to be with me, but I know that he'd be better off with Delilah."

"But you're his mother."

"And what do I say to him when he sees me doing a gangbang scene with three guys inside me at the same time? What can I do for him when his friends laugh and call his mother a whore?"

"You love him and tell him that you made mistakes. You tell him the truth and he will understand. Maybe not at first. But a boy will love his mother no matter what."

"I just don't feel like I belong," I said. "I thought when I had that orgasm on the set that that was the moment I could let go. I mean, I felt what it was like to be just a regular girl even through all that I'd done. But then I got home and Theon was dead and all our money was gone. I tried to go home but even there I didn't really fit. My mother feels guilty and even my brother Newland made me feel like some kind of alien."

"But I thought you two got along so well," Anna said.

"Yeah. He loves me but the life he's living has nothing to do with where I come from. We don't have anything in common.

"It's really only my brother Cornell whom I have any sympathy with. I understand why he hates me. I know in my heart that he'd feel better if I were dead. You can see it in the way he looks at me and in the way I look at myself in the mirror.

"I'm just fucked-up and there's no way I can undo it. There's no going back and I can't move ahead.

"You know how people say, 'He doesn't know what he's missing'?"

"Yes."

"The few friends I have would miss me if I was gone but they don't know me. They look at me and see something they need or want. They see somebody that they would rather be but I'm not even that woman. They'd miss me but they don't know who I am."

With that I had finished my truth telling for that morning.

While Anna was digesting the words I noticed a huge vulturelike bird perched on the roof of the office building across the street. At first I thought that it might be a statue, some kind of public art piece, but then it shifted.

I worried that maybe the bird was a hallucination, that if I pointed it out it might give Anna reason to have me committed. I couldn't allow that — not when I was so close to understanding.

I glanced at the kind woman. She gave me a quizzical look. She realized that I was looking out the window. The bird, whatever it was (or wasn't), decided at that moment to spread its great wings and leap from the rooftop. It seemed to bounce on an invisible current of air. Anna turned to look but before she could the creature lifted up beyond our line of sight.

It was gone.

"What were you looking at?" the therapist asked.

"Nothing," I said, "just the empty roof."

"Were you thinking of jumping off?"

"No."

"Then what?"

"A big bird," I said, "might be on its way somewhere. It could have stopped there to rest and then gone on. That building wasn't put there for birds to rest on. It's civilized and humanized but the bird doesn't know any of that. She just knew she was tired and had to rest for a little while before going on to where her instincts told her."

"I'm worried about you, Sandra."

"You shouldn't be, Anna. I'm on my way. I've been places I don't belong and now I'm just moving on."

"I'd like to prescribe an antidepressant for you," she replied.

"If you think I need it — sure."

My acquiescence seemed to soothe her

worry. From there we talked about my father again and how bereft my whole family was at his death.

"It was like a bomb went off in the living room," I said, "and we were all suffering from shell shock from then on."

"Does Theon's death bring up these memories of your father?"

This question was simple and seemingly unobtrusive — at first. I considered it. Theon was an outlaw too, in his own way. I had loved him as women love men in the beginning.

But did his death compare to my father's? Was his stupid demise an echo of Aldo Peel's reckless existence?

My father was a warrior, I thought, while Theon was a pimp and a whore. I was that real or imagined bird on the roof across the street from the woman pretending to be me. And Anna was everybody else, recording the complex interrelationships of men and women out there beyond the definitions of who and what and how we should be.

Theon was what Dickens would have called a swollen boy with an engorged member as his cross to bear. Daddy was a street fighter searching for and finding his manhood in back alleys and barroom fights.

"Sandra?" Anna said.

I looked up and out the window expecting to see a whole flock of condors waiting for me to join them or feed them. But the rooftop was empty.

"I have to go," I said.

"What were you thinking?"

"I don't have any answers, Anna. You can call in the prescription to Beacher's Pharmacy in Pasadena. I'll pick it up when I get home."

Anna tried to continue our unwieldy conversation but I needed to leave. I stood up and waded through her questions to the door. Before I left I told her about the funeral and said that it would be good for her to come.

Driving back toward my home I got a call.

"Yes?"

"Sandra?"

"Hey, Rash. Are you coming to the funeral?"

"I am."

"Is there something wrong?"

"I told Annabella about you."

"Your girlfriend?"

"She's pretty mad. It kinda surprised me. I mean, for the last year or so she's been totally distracted and kept on telling me how things weren't working. Now it's like we were married and I was cheating on her."

"If you can't come I'll understand," I said.

"No," he said, "I want to be there with you, I mean for you. I need to be there."

"What if you lose Annabella?"

"Then I won't have to leave her."

Maybe I should have said something then. It seemed clear that Rash was using me as the element of change in his life. Rather than just telling Annabella that he wanted to leave he was presenting me as the reason. Maybe I should have said for him to go figure out his relationship with her before coming to me.

But I felt so far away from anything except the actions I had to take that I wasn't worried about my hapless suitor. Maybe I even felt a little complimented that a man working in the real world would leave a pretty UCLA grad student for me.

Anyway, I'd be dead soon and then Rash could use me as a memory.

"Okay," I said. "If you get there early we can talk before the ceremony."

I drove out to LeRoy's Chicken and Waffle House and ordered two full meals. I ate at an outside table, scanning the skies for that big bird. I didn't see it but, I thought, that didn't mean it wasn't there.

After eating I went to a big toy store in Santa Monica and bought Edison a boy's computer that had learning games and a place to keep his diary.

By the time I got home I was happy. There was a silly grin on my face and a lightness in my spirit that I hadn't felt since I was a little girl. I wasn't worried about leg breakers or bill collectors, letting down my family, or the loss of people I loved or might have loved.

Even my breathing was cheerful. The air felt good coming in and going out. My entire life had been leading to this moment. No one could take it away. I didn't have to run or hide or pretend I was somewhere else while a man shoved his nine-inch-long, four-inch-wide dick into my rectum.

The feeling I had was exactly the same as when a young girl falls in love. I was in love with the beauty of finality and I had Theon to thank for that.

I got three sheets of paper from the office desk and sat down to write the eulogy. I sat there for hours writing slowly and surely. I didn't cross out a word. I wrote the whole thing in medium blue ink from an old-fashioned ballpoint pen. It was a retractable that I had taken from a Best Western motel when we had used a room on the sly to shoot the final scene of *Debbie Does It All.*

It was well past midnight when I finished the tribute. I slid from the chair onto the carpeted floor and smiled at the ceiling. I closed my eyes and was instantly asleep.

That was the best night of sleep I ever had — ever. It was dreamless and seamless, dark and soft. Any lingering trepidations I had about death were dispersed by the peaceful ecstasy of those eight hours.

I still had a few sore spots from the beating Coco gave me but the pain would end. I felt sadness about Theon and my son, my mother, and others but I knew that the dead were gone and the living could go on without me — had been doing so for years.

It was a lovely, balmy morning. I went barefoot out upon the blue-green grass that Theon cultivated just outside our dinette. He shaded that small lawn from the summer sun and made sure that it was well watered and cooled even in the L.A. desert.

The spiky blades tickled my bare soles, exhilarating me. I was naked out there. No one could see me and that was fine.

I couldn't remember the last time that I had solitude. I mean, I'd been alone often enough, but to know that I didn't have to strip down and oil up, to take a preparatory enema for the afternoon shoot, to manicure every square inch of flesh, nail, and hair . . .

I bathed for an hour listening to Mingus, my father's absolute favorite musician. I used lavender bubble bath and thought about Perry Mendelson. While I was sitting there, luxuriating, it struck me that I hadn't turned on the security system. Maybe I was reminded because I might have heard something behind the jazz. The sound, I thought, might have registered without my awareness, because the moment I thought it Richard Ness walked into the bathroom — the same room where my husband had died with the child I could not save.

"Dick," I said, only mildly surprised.

"I told you I don't like people calling me that." He was wearing a shit-brown suit and a green Borsalino hat.

"And I said that I don't like you."

"You owe me money, bitch."

"I thought you sold the debt to Manetti?"

"He gave it back. He said that you had my money now and I'm here to collect. I came here to see your green or your red."

"How festive." I had to hold back to keep from laughing.

My obvious good humor disconcerted him.

"Why you got to be like that, Deb?" he said. "I don't want to hurt you."

"How can we ever come to an understanding if you lie to me, Dick?"

"Say what?"

"You want to hurt me but you know if I die Jude Lyon will be unhappy. And if he's unhappy you might get damaged."

"This doesn't have anything to do with him," he said.

"But it does, sweetheart. It has to. You're mad and you're scared, so you came here to bully me to show that you can't be bossed around."

I'd hit the bull's-eye on Ness's shame. He grimaced and considered mayhem.

"You know I'm gonna have to kill you," he said.

"I know that you want to, Dick. The only question is if you're brave enough to murder an unarmed woman in her bath."

He was like a lover who couldn't perform. Everything but Dick's dick was willing. He sat down on the toilet seat and glowered at me.

"You are one crazy bitch."

"Yeah."

Warm steam was rising from my tub. My

breath was still magical.

"I'm gonna go through your house and take enough stuff to make my nut offa Theon."

"Be my guest," I said. "I don't own this house or anything in it. I don't want it, and besides, Theon has everything in hock. Take it all, Dick. I don't care about it or you. You can take everything, but I will call the cops and tell 'em you did it. I sure will."

Ness stood up and took a pistol from a shit-brown pocket. It was a small revolver made to look even smaller by his big hand. He pulled back the hammer as I had done with him a few mornings before.

I smiled and then grinned.

"You know what I'm gonna do, right?" he said.

I fluttered my eyelashes at him. It was the pretense of innocence that I'd used in a dozen films where I was some chaste child about to be indoctrinated into a brutal carnal world.

Dick raised his arm, leveled the pistol.

He fired. It sounded like a cap gun. Shards of shattered tile pelted my left shoulder from behind.

"You missed," I told him.

He fired again, this time to my right.

"Maybe you should get a little closer, Dick."

I fully expected to die in that same bathtub where my husband expired, in the place where Jolie Wins had electrocuted them both. I could have saved myself. I could have begged. I had the money for Ness in the trunk of my car. I didn't need it. But I wasn't going to give in. He would have to kill me and I didn't give a damn.

Dick's face, already crushed from a lifetime of angry blows, fell in on itself. He lowered the pistol and shook his head.

I wondered if he was looking inside himself for the strength to murder me. I had given him enough reason, enough disrespect. But he just turned around and walked out of the bathroom. I had no idea of the content of the chain reaction of emotions set off inside him.

It was late in the afternoon before I was ready to go out again. I drove my Jaguar down to Threadley Brothers Mortuary. Talia Dean was sitting at the stone desk.

Talia was young and waiflike. Her loose tie-dyed hippie dress and white sandals made her an anomaly in the house of the dead. But there was something perfect about that odd juxtaposition of intense life moving among the shadows of death.

"Hello, Mrs. Pinkney," the young woman said.

She rose and came around the marble slab to shake my hand. After this friendly and oddly perfunctory welcome she leaned forward and hugged me.

"I'm so sorry," she whispered in my ear.

Then she leaned back and stared into my eyes.

I tried to smile at her. Maybe I succeeded.

"Lewis is downstairs with your husband," brown-haired Talia said. "I can call him and ask if he's ready for you to come down."

I nodded. We both went to sit at the Fred Flintstone desk. While she pressed the right buttons to get to Lewis, my red phone rang.

"Hello," I said.

"Lewis?" Talia said on her line.

"Sandra?" Marcia Pinkney said over the red phone.

"Can Mrs. Pinkney come down to view her husband?" Talia asked.

"I decided to take you up on your offer," Marcia said.

"She's right here," Talia said.

". . . to come and see Theon," Marcia concluded.

I gave Marcia the address of the mortuary while Talia hung up and waited.

After I disconnected the call the displaced hippie said, "I can take you down to see your husband now, Mrs. Pinkney."

He was wearing a tan suit with his favorite Stetson in the coffin. I realized that Lana must have helped them get the clothes. I came into the cool, dark chamber alone. Talia had left me at the door.

Lewis was standing over the earthly remains of my poor lost husband. Theon was smiling. It was his natural smile. I had never before seen a corpse made to look as the person had in life.

Dardanelle had done a brilliant job.

"He looks just like Theon," I said.

"It was as if he did the work himself," Lewis told me. "The muscles of his face found that smile with the smallest urging. He was a man who enjoyed life."

"Every minute," I said, "like he was going to die the next day."

"In my business you learn to take advantage of the span you're allotted," the undertaker told me. "We see so many who fall before their time."

It was a simple pine coffin, unfinished as I had wanted it to be. Seeing him there I felt the emptiness created by his absence. It wasn't so much that I missed him but that he had been there in ways that no one else ever could. Now, for the next two days at least, I would be alone.

"Could you bring a cot in here?" I asked the lanky mortician. "I'd like to spend the last night at his side."

"That's against policy."

"Does that mean no?"

It was a simple canvas cot with X-crossed wooden legs at either end. The blanket was army surplus and very scratchy but that wouldn't interrupt my sleep. I sat there next to my dead husband, thinking that he would have been happy that I didn't have a book. The light in the small interment room was no more than forty watts — I wouldn't have been able to read anyway.

It would have also made Theon happy if I decided to have sex with him one more time before he went into the grave. At some younger, wilder time I might have given him that last good-bye.

But that night I just sat there feeling so at ease and comfortable.

I was considering taking off my dress and lying down when a knock came on the door.

I thought it was an overly formal Dardanelle, but when I pulled the door open Marcia Pinkney stood there. I had forgotten her completely.

That night she was wearing a black dress and a dark gray hat with a gray, loose-net veil. Her eyes were still shocking in their intensity but the wan smile she had from days before had been put away.

"Is he here?" she asked.

I stepped to the side, ushering her in with the movement. Her gait was stiff-legged; so much so that I stayed close to her side in case she stumbled.

The pine coffin reminded me of Queequeg's coffin in *Moby Dick* — the passage of death that also made room for life.

"Oh my God," Marcia said, standing over her son.

I put my arm around her shoulder.

She reached out and wept silently. I imagined that her tears would have felt hot.

"I treated him like a dog," she muttered.

"He acted like a dog, Marcia. That's why I loved him."

"You did?"

"Yes, ma'am."

"Even after all he did to you?"

"Of all the doors I could have run through, his was the kindest. He never hit me and he always listened — even when he didn't understand."

"I could have helped you buy a better coffin," she said.

"Come sit on the cot, Marcia."

The coffin was set on the floor and so when we sat on the makeshift bed we could look down upon Marcia's dead son's smiling countenance.

"He looks very natural," Marcia said. "I guess that sounds clichéd but it's true."

"You couldn't have stopped this from happening," I said. "I was his wife and I couldn't do it. Theon was after something that he could never have and he was gonna push it to the limit until he went off the side."

"But it was my fault."

"You can't look at it like that, Marcia. Theon was a man. You have to respect a man to live his own life, and if you do that then you have to let him be responsible."

"But I'm his mother."

"So let it hurt you that he's gone. Feel the pain of his death but don't climb in there with him."

The old woman took me in a feeble embrace. She cried on my arm and shook in gratitude and despair. She patted my hand and whispered my name, my real name.

After all that, she leaned away and said, "Thank you. I didn't do anything to deserve your kindness."

She left soon after. I didn't accompany her because I knew that Lewis would see her to her car. I was relieved to be alone again. Marcia's emotions were too intense for death.

In the cool light, on the stiff cot next to my dead husband, life slowed down to a reasonable pace. The death chamber was cool and sedate. There were no sounds from anywhere.

If I glanced to my right I saw Theon's smiling visage. For days I'd been hearing his voice on and off. But now that I was lying there next to him the words ceased. He was dead. I was as good as dead.

Drifting into sleep I was in the coffin with him. We were floating on a calm sea in the bright sun. We were both dead but Theon had accepted his passing and no longer had to look or think or guess. Our passage was uneventful, would always be. But for some reason I didn't get bored or restless. Theon's natural smile and the gentle sway of the coffin-boat on the water lulled any desire. . . .

"Mrs. Pinkney," Lewis Dardanelle said. He was shaking my shoulder gently.

I was naked on top of the coarse army

blanket. This didn't disturb me. I had spent my entire adult life naked in front of men, and women.

And I was like all the other naked bodies Lewis dealt with every day of his life. They were all dead, of course, but I was on that cusp too. Maybe Lewis intuited my nearness to death. I stood up, retrieved my dress from the end of the cot, and put it on.

"It's late," he said. "You have a visitor."

"What time is it?"

"Eleven."

"Oh my God," I said, remembering the same words issuing from Theon's mom. "Who's here?"

"She says that her name is Bertha Blueblood."

"Hey, Deb," the plump makeup artist and wardrobe designer said as she rolled her portable closet into the vault.

"Hi, B."

"Oh," she said when she saw Theon. "Wow. He looks really good. I guess that creepy old Dardanelle knows what he's doing."

She glanced at the cot and my rumpled dress but didn't say anything.

She opened the movable closet and said, "It's pretty dark in here but I got a light panel in the trunk. Let's plug in and get to work."

At twelve fifteen I walked out of Threadley Brothers Mortuary. My white satin dress matched the ass-length platinum blond wig, and my glasslike coral-tinted high heels lifted me five inches off the ground. My eyes were cobalt blue and I showed enough cleavage to have made Jayne Mansfield blush.

Lewis Dardanelle opened the back door to the pink stretch Cadillac limousine. Bertha got in first and I followed. Theon had already been loaded into the black hearse and was on his way to a final restlessness.

"Baby, you look great," Bertha said when the car left the curb.

"Theon would have wanted this," I said. "It's the least I could do."

When we got to the cemetery, located halfway between L.A. proper and the Valley, it was just a few minutes shy of one o'clock. Rash Vineland, in a shabby but becoming ash-colored suit, stood out in front of the chapel waiting.

He didn't recognize me at first. I smiled at his looking around my tightfitting dress to see if his friend was going to climb out of the car.

"Aren't you going to say hello, Rash?" I asked him.

"Sandy?"

"This is my friend Bertha. She did my clothes."

"Hi," he said to the wardrobe mistress.

She smiled at him and shook his hand.

Inside, the chapel was empty. There was a high podium and Theon's coffin sat before it. The hundreds of seats were vacant except for the little pamphlets with Theon's picture and the details of his life. I picked up one for his mother when, and if, I saw her again.

The room was appropriately empty and silent.

Rash was looking down on Theon.

"He looks very manly," he said to me.

"He was just a boy in his heart," I said. "Like my father and most other men."

This pronouncement caused Rash to lower his head and once again I felt like kissing him.

And once again I did not kiss him.

"Does your girlfriend know you're here?" I asked instead.

"I told her that I was coming," he said. "I even told her that she could come along but she said that if I went that I shouldn't come back."

"Why put yourself through all that?" I asked. "Why not just stay where you are?"

"Because I . . . I . . ."

"What?"

"I looked you up on the Net."

"My films?"

"No. They cost money. It was just a lot of parties and some famous people you've been seen with."

"If you want to know something you should ask me," I said. "And just so you'll know — I got dressed like I used to because Theon would have liked it. This is the last time I'll ever be seen like this."

"You sound angry."

It was true. I could hear the rage in my voice, feel it in my shoulders and balled-up fists.

"It's okay," I told the young architect. "I'm not mad at you. It's just the last time I'm playing the role of Debbie Dare and it weighs on me."

"You talk like a completely different person."

"And what do you think about her?"

"I'd, I'd build her a house in the woods if she'd come live with me there." I could tell that he'd been practicing those words.

303

"What if she got fat and ugly?"

"I don't care about how you look."

"What if I only came in the summer months and spent the rest of the year doing . . . I don't know . . . other things?"

He nodded his acceptance of my "what if" demands. I felt a hard knot rise up in my esophagus.

"I have to go, Rash. Can we talk about this some other time?"

"I'm sorry. I know this is the wrong place."

I turned away from my awkward suitor and approached the pulpit where Lewis Dardanelle stood wearing his forty-year-old tuxedo. He'd worn that outfit to thousands of funerals. Death permeated every fiber.

"Everything is ready, Mrs. Pinkney," the tall man assured me. "The caterers are at your home and Talia made sure that everyone who donated has an invitation. I have only one question."

I'd never liked Lewis. His demeanor was so practiced as to be synthetic. But now I saw something inside the man: an empathy that seemed to exist only for me.

"What do you want to know?" I asked.

"Who will you want as pallbearers?"

"My brother Newland," I said immediately, "and Jude Lyon because Jude was Theon's closest friend. If Myron Palmer comes he'd be a good choice because they, they're kind of the same. Neelo Brown can be my special representative and then Kip Rhinehart and Chas Mintoff. All you need is six, right?"

The undertaker smiled and lowered his head in a half nod.

"Anything else, Lewis?"

"I assume that you won't be having a religious ceremony."

I smiled and said, "No. No minister is coming."

"So what will be the order of speakers?"

"I'd like you to say a few words."

"Me?"

"I know that Theon would come down to Threadley's sometimes to see you. I have no idea what you guys used to do, but I know he came home in a cab as many times as he drove."

"I'd be honored," Dardanelle said.

"Then you could introduce Jude Lyon. I'll be the last speaker, after that."

"I'll make sure that Mr. Lyon sits up front with you."

As Dardanelle walked away a voice said, "Let me take a look at you, hon."

It was Bertha. She came at me holding a palette of various kinds of makeup.

"Sit down so I can get to your face, Miss

305

Amazon," she said.

She worked on my forehead and cheeks, lips and neck. She ran a comb through my fake hair and then looked me over.

"How do I look?"

"Just like Theon would'a wanted you to."

Flower arrangements had arrived by the dozens. Huge frames of every color and kind. These concealed the seats next to the podium and I went back there to hide from the growing crowd.

The mourners were filing in by then. You could hear the din of their conversation and sporadic laughter. The people who attended the funerals of our kind were given to laughter and tears, alcohol and drugs, violent outbursts and deep depression.

It was not unusual for a suicide or two to come in the wake of any event like Theon's.

They would be well dressed, some scantily so, as everyone would want to be seen as well as pay their respects. Funerals for our crowd were literal celebrations, like the primitive peoples of Europe reveling in life and death before a dour Christian God stripped them of their phallic symbols and painted faces.

I caught glimpses of them through the

heavy foliage. The dominant theme was black cloth and cleavage but there was a good deal of pink and scarlet and white. There was a lot of kissing and hugging and holding on. Two film crews took over the back of the chapel. The back row, in front of the cameras, was occupied by a dozen well-known porn directors.

I could see no toddlers or children. There were a few babies in young women's arms. Maybe one or two of them belonged to Theon. He'd once bragged to me that he'd fathered a child of every race on the planet.

Beethoven's Seventh Symphony was playing. Lewis knew Theon well enough that he didn't have to ask me about the music.

I was secure behind that hedge of memorial offerings and yet still had a feeling of belonging. The service was like a going away party for both Theon and me. By then I had definitely decided to use my father's pistol to kill myself in the creditors' house after the wake for my husband. The feeling of comradeship and certain death caressed me and the world was right — for once.

"Hey, Deb," Jude Lyon said. He was wearing a beautifully tailored medium gray suit with a bluish shirt and a scarlet-and-royal-blue tie.

"You look good, Jude."

"Every time Theon saw this suit he asked for my tailor's name."

The little assassin sat down next to me. He grabbed my hand with unexpected strength and said, "I know this must be hard for you."

"It's the life we lived."

"Have you had any more problems?"

That was the first time I realized that I had not called the cops on Ness. He had come into my house and shot at me. But it meant nothing.

"No," I said. "I think that little talk you had with Coco settled it all."

"Call me if you have any more trouble," he said. "That's the very least I can do."

I could see in his eyes that Jude was nervous. He had a folded piece of paper gripped in the fingers of his left hand — the speech no doubt.

When I put my free hand on his he shuddered.

"It's okay, Jude," I said. "This is what he would have wanted you to do."

An inquisitive light came into the college-educated killer's eye.

"Do you understand who I am, Deb?"

"I don't understand a damn thing, J. All I know is that I have to keep on movin' forward and for this little stretch of road you and me are on it together."

I could tell he wanted to say something, just a sentence of agreement or harmony, but instead Jude put his head down and let it bounce in a little nod.

The crowd was getting louder. Bold men and saucy women were sharing memories and despair. The chatter seemed to be an attempt at holding off the silence that was so deep inside that chapel.

The chapel was almost as large as the Rock of Ages House of Worship where my family prayed — but the big church at Day's Rest was a house of Death, not hope. The only reason people gathered there was because someone had died. There were no Sunday school lessons or weddings in this place. The transient parishioners bellowed and laughed, keened and cried to keep off the extraordinary quietude and the inescapable reality that no proper house of worship could ever really contain.

I closed my eyes and let the sounds of the mourners' words and laughter wash over me. Again I had the feeling of being far out at sea. I couldn't make out the individual words and sentences of the babbling gurgle, but I understood the meanings of the rising and lowering octaves.

All this brought a smile to my face.

"Are you ready, Mrs. Pinkney?" Lewis Dardanelle asked.

I opened my eyes, realizing that I had drifted into dreams while waiting for the service. It seemed so perfect that a chuckle escaped my lips.

Dardanelle was shocked and that pleased me. He was so used to being in charge of the final interment. Not only did he orchestrate but he knew every emotion and action that went through the minds of the principals. My nearly joyous ejaculation threw him off his game and that brought out a stronger laugh.

"Do you need a moment to collect yourself?" he asked, still flummoxed by the sudden lightness of my mood.

"Absolutely not."

Lewis turned away, walked out into the public eye, and took the few steps up to the podium. There was a control board up there that he used to turn the music down, but not off.

The clamor of the mourners lowered to hushed whispers.

The tall coffin banger (as he was sometimes referred to by the women who fucked him in his casket-bed) cleared his throat and the whispering stopped.

"I have been asked to say a few words before the next speakers," he said in his deep, soft voice. "This is unusual because I almost always represent the funeral home and not the deceased.

"But in this case the family is known to me. Theon Pinkney was a frequent client." Lewis stopped and showed a rare honest smile. "Not, of course, in his current state. No. Theon took care of his friends. If someone in his trade died penniless and alone, Theon brought them to me and paid for the services. If some poor bereft mother or daughter or spouse could not handle the work it takes to make the transition, Theon was there to lend a hand. He knew as much about this business as I do. He knew about the embalming chemicals and brands of coffins, state and city ordinances, and the many denominations that would and would not speak for the dead.

"This of course refers to Theon only as far as my business life goes. Most of you know me. The only role any, or at least most of you, have seen me fill is the funeral director — the undertaker who takes your loved ones away."

Lewis stopped there for a good quarter of a minute. I believe a real emotion was passing through him, a memory of someone he was or might have been.

"But Theon knew me in other ways. Sometimes he'd wake up in the middle of the night and call me at the mortuary. 'Hey, Lew,' he'd say, 'what you doin' down there tonight.' "

What shocked me was how much Lewis was able to sound like my husband.

"Often I was deep in my work," Dardanelle said, continuing, "but some nights I was just sitting around in the office. Theon would come over with a deck of cards and a bottle of . . . mineral water."

That got a few laughs. Theon always called cognac his mineral water.

"We'd play for matchsticks and drink, trading stories of what happened at work that day. We both practiced interesting trades."

More laugher.

"One evening I remember Theon telling me how he had to get on the set and stop a jealous lover from strangling his girlfriend on camera. The man was much bigger and more powerful than Theon, but he wouldn't let that young girl die. . . ."

Lewis was referring to Tina Bottoms — at least, that was her screen name. Her boyfriend, who went only by the moniker Turk, had gotten it into his head to immortalize them both by killing her on film.

Turk broke Theon's arm, jaw, and ankle, but my husband saved that girl and helped her move back to Amherst, Massachusetts, where she'd been born.

"He was a good man and he treated me as a friend," Lewis said. "He never made fun of me or my predilections, and he loved his wife. I will think of him every time work slows down and I am sitting at my desk wondering what is it that I'm missing."

Again there was silence from the podium. That stillness seemed to fill the great hall of death. At least thirty seconds passed before the undertaker could bring himself to speak again.

"There will be only two other speakers at this service. The first will be the deceased's good friend Jude Lyon. Mr. Lyon will be followed by Theon's wife, Sandra Peel-Pinkney.

"Those of you who donated to this service have already been informed about where the wake will be held. There you will each be given a chance to drink mineral water and toast the dead."

Dardanelle walked away from the podium and down into the pews. A few seconds passed and the audience began to shift in their seats. I was moved by the friendship

Lewis evinced in those few words. It showed me something about Theon that I knew but rarely witnessed — he was a good friend to a certain kind of man: an outcast who had something to offer but with few takers. He felt comfortable with people like Jude and Lewis, and with him, they belonged.

Something was wrong. I went through all the things I knew at that moment, trying to find out what had misfired. I was dressed the way I should be. The room was full of Theon's friends. Rash was in the audience. . . .

"Jude," I said. "Jude."

I reached out to touch his arm but he grabbed my wrist before I could. His grip was hard.

"You have to go up there, baby," I said.

He gazed in my eye. He was an angry child caught in his own conflicting desires.

Then he let me go, jumped to his feet, and scurried out onto the dais. He tripped on the first stair, caught himself, and then stepped slowly up to the podium.

Lewis had adjusted the microphone for his great height and so Jude brought it down and twisted the snakelike metal stalk until the little receiver was there at his lips.

He cleared his throat and looked around.

He turned to me and I gave him my best smile.

He turned back to the audience and then remembered the folded-up paper in his hand. This he unfolded and placed on the podium before him. Then, for an uncomfortable span of time, he read the words silently to himself. I wondered if he thought that he was reading out loud and the assembly could hear him.

I was about to get up and go out to him when he raised his head.

"Theon Pinkney was my best friend," he said in a voice that was flinty and certain. "I don't really know what I meant to him but he was my best, best friend."

Jude splayed out his right hand over his chest. I thought that this was maybe the only time I'd seen the real man.

"Person of interest," he said then. "That's what I've been called many times. A person of interest. That's not a good thing, not at all. I mean . . . it's good for the person who others are interested in insofar as it's good that they're interested, because that makes you special — unique. But at the same time" — I realized then that Jude was not reading from the creased page in front of him — "it means that there's a whole world out there wanting to tear you down. They want to catch you, imprison you, maybe even take your life. A man," he said, and then he glanced at me, "or a woman who rises to the level of interest is something special. While everyone else is following canned music they're moving away, looking for their own.

"Theon Pinkney was a person of interest. He had a big stomach, a big heart, and a big dick" — a laugh or two came from the hall of death — "and he didn't care who knew it. He'd take off his clothes in a minute and lick his lips after throwing back a big slug of brandy. He was afraid of death; I know that because like Mr. Dardanelle, death is my stock-in-trade. Theon was afraid of dying but being fearless in the face of death isn't much. It isn't anything. The thing I loved about Theon was that he wasn't afraid of tomorrow. When the sun came up he looked around to see what there was on the horizon. He'd watch a ball game and then go to his mother's church when he knew she wouldn't be there. He flew off to Morocco the day after nine-eleven to see if the world looked different.

"Another thing about Theon was that he was a natural-born filmmaker. Not like these Hollywood fools with their automatic robots and ridiculous, impossible love stories. Theon saw the world he lived in today, the world we all live in. He knew what people wanted and what exhilarated them. He knew what you needed even when you didn't.

"No one has ever touched my life the way he did. And I'm sorry he's dead but I am happier, by far, that he lived."

Jude turned away from the podium and paused for a moment to make sure that he didn't tumble down the stairs. He walked stiff-legged back to his chair, where he sat down and bowed his head.

Lewis recorded every word spoken at the podium. For the first time I was happy about that. I wanted the words that Jude spoke to live on.

I waited for the pulse of Jude's speech to pass and then I walked out onto the stage with my ass-length platinum hair and fiery cobalt eyes, in five-inch coral heels. I stalked up to that podium like I was going to do the salsa with it. I pulled on that micro-phone until it reached my lips and I touched the off-center white bull's-eye inside the faux tattoo on my cheek. My nostrils flared and the chill of the room braced my black skin. Whenever I moved I heard the white satin slide against my body, and I was home — if only for a moment.

"All my years with Theon have brought me to this place," I said. "It was like he was driving here from a million miles away and stopped to pick me up on the side of the road. 'What's this little black girl doin' out here?' he said when he saw me. 'Anything you want, Daddy.' And ever since then we've been together. I was his tenant, his costar, his girlfriend, and his wife. He loved me and hated me and stomped out the front door more times than I can count. He's fucked more women than any basketball player or U.S. senator. He's crossed almost every line that they put down in church.

"I went with him willingly but I hate where I've ended up. I love the people in this room but I can't stand what we do to each other. It's not like I think we're less than the people who live out in the straight world buying our videos and looking to see if we bleed. We're better than them because we know that there's no difference between men and women, black and white, Christian and Jew, young and old.

"We know better but that's not enough. We pay for that knowledge with drug addiction and STDs. We suffer from the people who feel alive only when watching our asses on electronic screens. We are beaten and raped and spit on. They pay us for this and

318

we smile our bloody smiles and learn to pretend even when we know better."

That wasn't my speech. I had yet to unfold the papers in front of me. That was merely my recognition of the familiar faces in that room. I'd had sex with at least half of them.

"But none of that is why I'm here. I mean, I do love you. We have blazed a trail across the imagination of the world. They may not like it, they might not like us, but here we are, bound together to say good-bye to one of our own.

"We've come here to celebrate him, but Theon has been the star before. In movies, behind the camera, on the red carpet, and winning every award they have to offer. I don't mean Theon but Axel Rod — the self-proclaimed hardest-working cock in the Valley."

That got me some grins and guffaws.

"Theon was an imperfect man in an imperfect world," I continued. "A child died on his lap. A little girl, barely sixteen. All she had was the beauty of youth and the desire and the willingness to climb out of the shit of her childhood. She died fucking my husband in our big bathtub and he died reaching for her, because in her fractured youth he saw himself just like he saw himself

319

in me when I was her age.

"She was born Myrtle May but she called herself Jolie Wins."

I gazed around the great chamber and saw that every eye was on me. That brought a smile to my lips, not because I needed to be the center of attention but because that was a tough crowd and you had to tell the truth to keep their interest.

"When I met her I was looking at her backside and she was on her knees in front of some fat wannabe. She was high and didn't even know where she was. She called me miss and asked me to help her. I tried. I did. But, as we all know, there's no help for the likes of us.

"Her story was the same old, same old — her panties and Daddy's dick, Mother making noise in another part of the trailer, and the sun shining outside just like nothing ever happened. In a lot of rooms words like that would call up tears and indignation, but in here we've all heard it and felt it one way or another.

"I took her by the hand and brought her to what I thought was a safe harbor. I gave her my private number and a promise I could not keep.

"She and Theon found each other and saw in each other's eyes the dreams that they always had. They grabbed at each other, not for sex or solace but for hope. They were outlaws on the run just like the rest of us.

"And I believe that Mr. Dardanelle and Jude are outlaws too. I believe that Theon would want us to remember them and Myrtle May, because he did have a big heart and he wanted something that he knew he could not have, but that never kept him from trying.

"We are that something. We are the scenes on the wide-screen plasma TVs that millions watch every night hoping for something that they can never have. They stay in their condos and trailers. They go to work and talk about the newest cop show but that's not what they're feeling.

"Myrtle May left home when she was just a child. She died still a child. Theon was so lost that he might have even thought that he was helping her. He thought that he had saved me — I did too. But that was never true. We aren't in the saving business. We are down-to-the-bone serious and at risk. We are, and Theon was, all the pain that happens on the back alleyway that leads between the bank doors and the church.

"And so I am here in the persona of Debbie Dare to tell you what Theon should have said to Myrtle May.

"Save yourself. Know that you can do anything. Don't look down on anyone. Don't forgive them or condemn them. And when they tell you to get down on your knees, you tell them to get down there with you. Tell them that you can take the pain if they will too."

What happened immediately after those last words is a blur to me. I think I just stood there staring for a while until Jude came up and led me off the stage. From there Lewis brought me to the side of the coffin, where I was joined by Lana Leer. She was wearing a simple black dress that went down to her calves and was shod in white pumps.

I came to myself standing there next to the open coffin. Theon still looked natural, almost as if he might open his eyes at any moment.

"That was a beautiful eulogy," Lana whispered.

"I never got to the words I'd written," I said. "I just kinda got lost up there."

"It was still wonderful," my little friend said. "It touched a lot of people. You gave 'em a lot to think about."

Lewis had gone out among the mourners and was lining them up along the left side of the pews.

"Are you ready?" Lana asked.

"Ready for what?"

"For the people to walk by and pay their final respects."

"Oh." For some reason this responsibility had escaped me. "Sure."

Moana Bone was the first in line. Her once fine features were heavy, made more so by an overabundance of makeup. Her body had thickened to the point where she had no real figure anymore.

With surprising strength she gripped my hands and said, "I'm very sorry for you, my dear. What you said up there is in the hearts of all us whores. We do the heavy lifting and they flush us down anyway."

"Do you know my name?" I asked, feeling numb and reckless.

"They call you Debbie Dare in the cast list, but your real name is Sandra Peel. I always loved Theon but you were better for him than I could have ever been."

Her eyes were on mine like some kind of emotional predator tracking down a simple nod.

"Hey, Deb," Myron Palmer said after Moana wandered off. Standing next to him was a mousy woman wearing a loose, dark green shift. Her face was once pretty and her gestures recalled that younger beauty.

"I wanted to thank you for letting me be a pallbearer," Myron said. "You know, I really liked Theon and, and, and I styled myself after him as much as I could."

"Thank you, Myron."

I shook his hand, which was both soft and strong, and then offered the same gesture to the woman he was with. She took the proffered hand and said, "You have my condolences, Mrs. Pinkney."

"Have we met?"

"No. I'm Myron's friend Nora."

"Brathwait?"

"He told you about me?"

"You were the love of his life. I don't think he's had a single day where he hasn't thought of you."

"Your speech was beautiful," she said. "Myron and I have just reconnected over Facebook recently. I'm trying to get him to leave this profession and do something else — maybe still in film."

Our middle-aged Russian housekeeper, Julia Slatkin, came up after half an hour.

"I am so sorry for you, my child," she said.

"You didn't have to come to this zoo, Julia."

"I love you and your people," she said. "Theon was a good man. He was a man and so he was always a little lost. Men are like boys and sometimes the only thing we can do is put them to bed."

I hadn't even been worried about crying until she spoke those words.

"He did awful things," I said.

"And he has paid for them," she replied with Jude-like certainty. "There's only so much revenge that God can ask on any man's soul."

"Those were really nice words you spoke up there," hunched-over Kip Rhinehart said after what seemed like hours of pity and commiserations.

I was thinking of how lovely it would be to sit down in the polar bear room, bring my father's pistol (the pistol that failed to save his life) to my temple, and pull the trigger. . . .

"I heard," Kip, the canyon cowboy, went on, "that you're havin' money troubles and might not be able to make that mortgage. If that's so you're welcome to come up and live in one'a my rooms. It gets a little lonely up there and . . . and I wouldn't bother you or anything. I'm kinda old for that nonsense."

I was imagining the red spray across the white fabric that I chose to accent my ebony skin.

"You think about what I said," Kip muttered after I thanked him.

Linda Love came up with a small band of directors. They said the right words but didn't really mean them. A has-been actor was just that in their business. Neelo Brown shook my hand and kissed my cheek. He'd been an awkward adolescent — a virgin at eighteen. It was decided among his aunties that I would be the one to initiate him into the sexual life. I took him down to Ensenada for his birthday and came into his room after a night of dinner and trying to teach him how to dance. I did it to build his confidence but after that he was always a little in love with me.

Anna Karin, Newly, Perry Mendelson, Chas and Darla the accountants, and my son's guardian, Delilah, came up singularly and in pairs. All the while I was thinking about Suicide — that handsome man who joined me every once in a while, all silence and smiles.

Toward the end of the procession two men wearing identical suits and faces approached me. They were pale and thin, of equal and normal height, but still they seemed small. Their eyes were barely gray and their lips . . . non-existent. The one on the left walked up to me and took my hand. "John," he said, and then moved my hand to his brother, who said, "Ronald."

"Threadley," they both said together. It was like a routine from an old-time vaudeville act.

"We rarely involve ourselves with the day-to-day," Ronald said.

"But we felt driven to come here and say our good-byes to your husband," John added.

"It's not the business he brought us," Ronald said.

". . . but his belief in our ability to provide the requisite care," the brother added.

I wondered which one was born first and if they'd die on the same day.

I thanked them and smiled for them. I almost told them that we'd be seeing each other soon.

Before the coffin was sealed I tucked Myrtle May's unopened diary next to Theon's heart. The night-blue-and-chrome hearse was parked outside. People had been drifting away toward the burial site. It was up on a hill, I was told, a place where anyone visiting could look out on the faraway mountains or down on the valley where Theon grunted and strained and came on command.

Almost everyone had gone. I was standing in front of the chapel waiting for Lewis to come with a car for me. The Threadley brothers were there, and Lana too.

I felt the weight of the past week or so lift from me. The day was sunny and gorgeous. I said good-bye to the world then and there. It would be my last day and that was a deep relief.

I could finally let go.

"Bitch!" a woman yelled.

I turned to my right. A light-skinned black woman wearing jeans and a pink blouse was rushing at me. There was something in her hand. I knew immediately what was happening. The woman was certainly Annabella Atoll, Rash's girlfriend. She had, I imagined, come from a background like mine and saw Rash as a good partner to move away from what she was. He saw in her a life that he had missed, but when she sloughed off the old skin he lost interest and then met me.

The knife arced down across the left side of my face, slicing through skin and eye with razor-sharp accuracy. Then almost immediately came the upthrust under my right breast. There was pain but not that much.

The twins were amazing. One of them tackled Annabella. Her strength was fueled by hate-driven adrenaline, though, and she almost threw him off. But Lana grabbed something and hit my would-be killer in the head — twice. While my friend and one twin subdued Annabella, the other twin lowered me to the ground and applied pressure to the wounds.

I could hear my rasping breath and see Suicide just behind John — or maybe it was Ronald. There was screaming and hollering and I was back in the living room where my father stumbled in and died. My good eye was open wide; I knew this but saw nothing. The world around me was moving but I was absolutely still. This contradiction seemed like a great revelation to me.

Waking up in Neelo's clinic was not a big surprise, not really. There were oxygen tubes in my nostrils and other plastic hoses down my throat. My left eye was bandaged and a searing pain ran down that side of my face.

"Sandy?" Lana Leer said. She was looking down at me with fear in her eyes.

I tried to smile but I don't think she could tell.

"You're gonna be okay," she said in a voice

that was anything but certain. "They arrested that crazy bitch and put her in jail. Neelo says that your eye and lung got cut up pretty bad but —"

"That's enough for right now," Jude Lyon said, interrupting my chatterbox friend.

I turned to see his concerned countenance. The person of interest smiled at me. There was no promise in that smile but I felt his caring. I could see the coldness in his eyes beyond the everyday human attention. There was also an inkling I had that something had changed in the person he was seeing.

"Your friend the doctor is doing all that he can," Jude said. "That woman cut you up pretty bad but you're in good hands."

After that I passed into unconsciousness. For all intents and purposes I was dead.

When I awoke again the tubes were gone but my eye was still bandaged. Neelo came to see me soon after I'd regained consciousness.

"You're gonna be all right, Aunt Deb," he said, showing more relief than I felt. "It was tough going there for a while. We had to drain your lungs every day for three weeks and you were on life support for half that time. I'm actually surprised that you survived.

"I brought in seven specialists to operate on that eye. We still don't know how your vision will be affected. But you're gonna live, Aunt Deb. You know I love you. It would have killed me if you died."

After that day the visitors started coming. It was like Theon's death procession but over a greater length of time. Neelo's words stuck with me.

Rash didn't come but sent a note with Lana.

Dear Sandy,
I'm so sorry for the pain and danger I brought into your life. There are no excuses and I will not bother you again. I'm moving down to Miami next month and plan to start a little business down there with a guy I studied with at college. Please forgive me and try to forgive Annabella. She was just out of her head.
Rash

A few days later a woman lawyer named Katya Corvine came to get me to put on record that I was having an affair with Rash. I agreed and also documented that I bore no ill will toward my attacker.

■ ■ ■ ■

There was a noticeable scar down the left side of my face, and when the eye patch was removed I saw an odd double image out of that eye. My face in the mirror looked a little off because of my impaired vision and disfigurement. But to me it was all good. The wounds inflicted were like a surgeon's incisions, cutting out a deep, ancient infection.

I no longer wanted to die.

When Delilah and Edison were allowed in to see me I told my son that we would live together on a mountain overlooking the ocean.

"What about Mama Delilah?" my caring boy asked.

Kip Rhinehart had already agreed to all three of us living in his abandoned school.

"She can live with us as long as she wants."

Edison cheered. Delilah had already agreed.

Delilah and Edison drove me from the canyon and as soon as I was better I got a job as a waitress at a seafood house on the Pacific Coast Highway.

One day, a little more than a year after

Theon's funeral, Edison was sitting on my lap as we watched the sun settle into the Pacific. He ran a finger down the trail of the scar on my face.

"Does it hurt you, Mama?" he asked.

"No, baby," I said. "It reminds me."

"Of what?"

"When I feel it going down my face I think that it's a road my life took to this place."

"A scary road with ghosts?"

"No. It's just the way I had to go to get here with you."

"And Mama Delilah an' Uncle Kip," he added.

"Yes."

There was a seriousness beyond Eddie's tender years in his face. And farther than that, beyond this childhood wisdom, there was a lovely California sunset and I felt that I had arrived at a place where no one could bring me down on my knees.

ABOUT THE AUTHOR

Walter Mosley is the author of more than forty-one books, most notably twelve Easy Rawlins mysteries, the first of which, *Devil in a Blue Dress,* was made into an acclaimed film starring Denzel Washington. *Always Outnumbered* was an HBO film starring Laurence Fishburne, adapted from his first Socrates Fortlow novel. A native of Los Angeles and a graduate of Johnson State College, he lives in Brooklyn, New York. He is the winner of numerous awards, including an O. Henry Award, a Grammy Award, and PEN America's Lifetime Achievement Award.